SYZYGY

It was over quickly. The fish were leaping into the boat, the men standing, fighting them off. Fish trailed from the yellow sides, tearing at the fabric. The men were screaming as the boat out of control, veered in a tight circle, sank lower in the water, and spluttered to a halt as water entered the carburettor. They were about fifteen yards from the quay and there was nothing we could do to help . . .

Later, Arthur invited himself up to my place.

He said: 'I think we's better put our heads together over this thing. I was watching those fish. They seemed to be . . . . organized . . . .'

Michael G. Coney

SYZYGY

ARROW BOOKS

ARROW BOOKS LTD
3 Fitzroy Square, London W1

An imprint of the Hutchinson Publishing Group

London Melbourne Sydney Auckland
Wellington Johannesburg Cape Town
and agencies throughout the world

First published by
The Elmfield Press in association with
Shire Publications Ltd 1973
Arrow edition 1975

Made and printed in Great Britain
by the Anchor Press Ltd
Tiptree, Essex

ISBN 0 09 911020 2

PROLOGUE

One evening, about one Arcadian year before the onset of the Relay Effect, Sheila and I attended a dance in the Riverside Recreation Dome. The place was full—a jostling crowd of humanity determined to enjoy themselves, cavorting grimly to the imperfect beat of an inferior band. The Master of Ceremonies had been brought in especially for the occasion; he was, so we were informed, great fun—a genuine character who would make any party go. On hearing this I tried to make some excuse not to attend, but Sheila was insistent. Everybody, it appeared, was going; and it was tacitly understood that this was to be the beginning of a new relationship between the Research Station and the private colonists of Riverside.

At midnight the dance was at its peak, the band deafening, the trumpeter swaying and blasting in imminent danger of a coronary. I sat with Sheila at a side table drinking while she watched wistfully as the packed floor performed an old-fashioned dance from Scotland, on Earth. I did not know this dance. The rhythm irritated me. People jigged about in small circles, taking it in turns to move into the centre and perform.

One young man caught my eye; I watched with interest as he pranced on the circumference of his little group, his face pink and sweating, living this moment of great joy which would only be surpassed when he got into the middle of the circle. His chance came after two false starts, and he capered forward, arms upraised as though at gunpoint, leaping and posturing, all the while uttering falsetto yelps like a maimed dog. At last he retired, eyes bright, sweat streaming, and clapped rhythmically while a large woman attempted to emulate these antics. He fascinated me, this young man. I wondered what was motivating him—in his normal role he was an eminently serious young scientist at my Research Station.

The number ended, there was a burst of applause from the participants, the MC took the mike. He was a large dark man with an aggressive smile and a hypnotic manner. "Now, Ladies and Gentlemen!" he bellowed. He paused for that microsecond of time which arouses speculation, then confidently shouted: "It's the Snake! Everybody on the floor!"

Tumultuous approval. People began to writhe. I heard delighted cries of "Oh, the Snake!" as there was a mass exodus from the tables to the floor. They had forgotten the Scottish dance; they wanted to do the Snake. The Snake was the most. I felt Sheila tugging my hand, and looked up. Her eyes were glazed with anticipation; she was standing and obviously took it for granted that I wanted to do the Snake. Everyone loved the Snake . . .

I stood resignedly. I obediently began to writhe, slightly out of rhythm. I looked around, embarrassed, at everyone writhing. The pink young scientist was particularly happy; one complex manoeuvre took him almost to his knees.

I said sarcastically: "If they like the Snake so much, why not do it all night? Why bother with the other dances?"

Sheila stared at me uncomprehending, writhing.

ONE

The dark sea was quietly calm and the ripples touched with crimson by the terminal rays of the setting sun. In my hand the tiller was gently alive, nudged by the wavelets, quivering to the muted putter of the 5½ horse-power outboard. There was little wind, just a light kiss against our faces as Jane and I sat in companionable silence in the small cockpit of *Carousel*. Above us the boom swung idly to the lullaby rocking of the boat; the carelessly-rolled sail hung limp. I like the old-fashioned sailing boat; there is still a place for it despite the advantages, often described to me by Riverside fishermen, of the latest hover-trawlers, which they cannot themselves afford. It takes many generations for a new colony to attain Earth standards. . . .

To the south, the last of Arcadia's moons crept towards the horizon. "There goes Gimel", I observed. My voice was an anachronism in the evening quiet.

Jane turned and gazed after the small silver disc. "It's a strange feeling," she said. "I'm nineteen years old, and I've never known a moonless night. I can't imagine it. Just black. Nothing up there." A kite-bug—a tiny glowing beetle suspended from a triangular phosphorescent web—drifted past the masthead.

"There's always the stars," I reminded her.

"It's not the same thing. There's something so . . . final, seeing the last moon go down. As though everything was finished."

I laughed. Jane has a tendency toward an overactive imagination. "Remember, they can see all six moons on the other side of the world. And the moons will be overhead here, tomorrow. You may not see them in daylight, of course. But we'll know they're there . . ."

"You mean the tides?"

3

"I think we're ready for them."

Nevertheless I was concerned. Arcadia's moons describe erratic orbits: the phenomenon which would take place over the next few weeks occurred once every fifty-two years. We could only hope that all precautions had been taken. A further complication was the sketchiness of the records concerning the previous occurrence. I'm a fifth-generation Arcadian. The planet, nine-tenths water with a single equatorial continent and a few scattered islands, was colonized by Earth one hundred and thirty years ago. I am thirty-two years old and had not witnessed the unique grouping of the six moons before.

Some of the older members in the settlement of Riverside remembered it, but they were curiously reticent. All that was known was that inexplicable riots and drownings had taken place. Some of the elderly had ridiculous theories; they spoke of a werewolf effect—God knows who dreamed that idea up, but it certainly captured their imaginations. A few weeks earlier I had been talking to Jed Spark in the Social Club. He's sixty years old—third-generation Arcadian—and he speaks with an authority born of senility.

"It stands to reason," he said. "When you get all six moons lined up together its bound to affect folks' minds. There's a gravitations pull on the brain; it sends you queer. I remember—I was only a kid—the last time this happened it was Christmas or thereabouts. My folks gave me a present, a big parcel. I looked at it, and I looked at them, and suddenly I knew what was inside that wrapping. When I opened it up, I was right; it was an old-fashioned train set with a red engine, imported from Earth. It must have cost them a fortune. But that feeling of having looked right through the wrapping put me off a bit, I can tell you." He shivered dramatically and extorted a beer from me as compensation for mental distress.

At the time I had smiled, but a few weeks ago four men arrived at the Research Station. I knew one of them slightly, a man named Arthur Jenkins; I'd met him at a science convention nine months ago. Although our fields are poles apart we had enjoyed an interesting conversation during a particularly boring lecture. I am a marine biologist and he found the subject fascinating—but I've hardly seen him during this last two weeks.

Obviously Arthur and his men constitute some sort of team, and the subject of their investigations is being kept dark. One thing I do know—Arthur is a psychiatrist. Which suggests that they are investigating us, the people of Riverside, and our reaction to the fifty-two-year phenomenon. Oddly enough, it appears that the reaction, whatever it is, only occurred among people in the coastal areas. Oldhaven, our nearest large port, was burned to the ground; people were attacking their friends on sight, so it is said . . .

I watched idly as a vociferous flock of junkers disputed a fish one of their number had caught after a typically clumsy dive. Around them the tiny newlers hovered above the surface—marine humming-birds, their diet consists of plankton snatched from the sea in their pointed, needle-like bills.

I brought myself back to the present—Jane was speaking: They say the rise and fall is going to be over a hundred feet," she remarked. Under the normal scattered distribution of Arcadia's moons the tide is negligible.

"That's all right. We've got it all worked out. A few residents will have to evacuate to units on higher ground, and we've arranged temporary accommodation at the Research Centre, and with other people around there. After the tides have finished, we'll all go down and lend a hand cleaning out their units. It'll be a case of communal effort. I think everyone will help." Riverside has a population of about five hundred, of which about one-fifth are employed at the Station; the sub-colony is grouped at varying altitudes on the steep slopes at the head of the estuary. I expected about thirty units to be rendered uninhabitable for a period of at least two weeks—indeed, many of the lower-lying dwellings were already submerged at each tide.

"But what about the fish?" Jane asked.

This was a major problem. The private colonists of Riverside depend on fishing and agriculture for their income. At one time fishing was entirely carried on by a fleet of eight small trawlers; these still set off down the two-mile estuary every day, returning in the evening loaded to the gunwales. But five years ago I arrived on the scene and the Riverside Biological Research Station was set up. Our first project was to investigate the feasibility of fish farms along the lines of those on Earth. We have to move with the times; a colony cannot stagnate, technology-wise, despite the abundance of natural food resources on Arcadia. With a minimum budget and a wealth of local opposition I got the project under way, and there are now sixteen pens to the west of the estuary mouth covering an area of almost a thousand acres. I was now facing the biggest problem yet. At low tides the fish would be overcrowded and starving—the Arcadian fatty has a high metabolism—whereas at high tides they would be able to swim over the tops of the pens and thereby escape.

"We're going to feed them each high tide," I explained. "We motor over the tops of the pens and drop pellet fodder overboard. It sinks to the bottom. This will encourage the fatties to stay in the pens and feed from the ground. Even when the tide goes out and they get crowded, they'll still have plenty to eat."

"That's going to be a big job. How can we manage sixteen pens?"

"I've requisitioned the trawlers. They'll anchor at the mouth of the estuary, load up with fodder there and take it to the pens, scattering it like seed."

Jane laughed. "I don't suppose that'll make you very popular with the fishermen." The fishermen feel—and rightly—that the fish farm will eventually put them out of their jobs. This is the main reason for the undercurrent of feeling between the private colonists and the Research Station.

"They can't use the trawlers for anything else. Soon the estuary will dry out at each low tide, apart from a few pools. At high tide the ebb and flow will be so strong that they'll be risking their lives if they try to put to sea. I don't suppose they're sorry, really. And it gives them a chance to complain about the authorities, which is their favourite sport."

"So that's why you've been taking all that stuff along the track to the point. You had all this worked out months ago."

"I couldn't really say anything. Fortunately, the Riverside fishermen aren't far-sighted. If they'd known what I intended, they'd have applied for a grant to widen and concrete the track, and then trucked their fish from the point to the colony. It's too late now. It's as much as you can do to get a tractor along there with a trailer. It took me over a hundred journeys to accumulate the stockpile of fodder."

Jane fell silent. Her face was thoughtful in the light from the cabin, and I felt the familiar sickness of longing as once again I noted her resemblance to Sheila . . .

We were moving between the tall headlands at the estuary mouth; they appeared threatening, jagged in the unaccustomed gloom. The tide was receding fast, and *Carousel* made slow headway in the black swirling water. From the bows, a V wave of bright phosphorescence angled into the darkness.

"The water must be almost solid with plankton," I observed, forcing my mind free of unhappy memories. The mewlers were all over the water, feeding rapidly and uttering piping cries.

"I'd noticed that. It seems that the things stay in the creek, whatever the state of the tide. At low water the channel's like soup. Billions of them, fighting the ebb. There seem to be more every night."

Around the boat were other ripples—blue, fast-moving trails with the occasional glimpse of a triangular fin. "Blackfish too," I said. "They seem to be gathering in the creek. I hope they don't get into the pens."

The blackfish is the Arcadian equivalent of the terrestrial shark, Slim, swift and incredibly ferocious, they prey on the fatties and are the bane of the trawler fishermen, ripping the nets to shreds with their needle teeth. A blackfish at large in one of my pens can decimate the fatty population in a few hours. They kill instantly, sinking their teeth into their prey immediately behind the head, then moving on to the next without a pause. They kill indiscriminately, blindly, apparently for the fun of it, pausing to eat only rarely. The fishermen wear girdles of soluble repellent when at sea; the solution is not always effective . . . As I watched a blackfish rose in a glittering leap, snatched a hovering mewler and sank beneath the surface again.

The last faint reflections of Gimel were silvering the mud-flats as we drove up the final mile, the engine labouring in the swift current, the air salty with stranded plankton and acrid with petrol fumes. On either side the gathering hills bulked black, relieved directly ahead by the friendly lights of the colony. I began to think of the warm atmosphere of the Social Club and the cool clean tang of beer.

I eased the tiller over, following the channel. It swung to the right, close beside a steep rocky stretch of shore where, decades

ago, a section of the rugged outcrop at the top of the long ridge
had broken loose and tumbled down to the water's edge to lie
in heaped, meaningless confusion. Time had softened the bleak
stone; moss clung to the boulders, and lower down, seaweed.
Gnarled trees had crept determinedly among them, in places
right to the river's edge, where they dipped tentative toes into
the water from the security of stances dry at any normal state
of the tide. For the next few weeks, however, these trees would
find their position dangerous, as the rising water drowned even
their topmost leaves. In a month's time they would be irrevo-
cably poisoned by the saline tide and, later in the year, would
topple across the water, breaking loose from their roots, to
drift against the steep bank and lie there half-submerged, like . . .

"Don't think about her, Mark."

I jumped stupidly, startled by Jane's sudden command.
"How . . . ?" My involuntary question petered out. I knew how
she knew.

"You always do. Whenever we pass Anchor Pool in the dark
you think of Sheila. It's time you thought of somebody else.
There are plenty of nice girls in the colony. Stop being a hermit
and get around a bit, go to dances and things. It's no use
spending your evenings in the Social Club and your mornings
sleeping it off. At first you were sorry because of her, but now
you've become more sorry for yourself. I'm sorry too; after all,
she was my sister. But I've got over it. It's about time you got
over it too."

I stared at her. I was astonished at the vehemence of her
outburst, which seemed in rather bad taste. She was gazing
grimly up the creek, and the cabin light emphasized the determined set of her round chin, Sheila's chin . . . But Sheila's hair
had been shoulder-length and blonde, whereas Jane's was short
and auburn. And their personalities were quite different, Sheila's
easy-going charm contrasting sharply with Jane's forthright,
sometimes crude, down-to-earth attitude.

"I was in love with her," I said mildly and sadly, conscious
that I was acting, that I was trying to shut her up by appealing
to her sympathy.

"So fall in love again," she retorted roughly, unabashed.
"You've proved it can be done."

We were passing the first of the Riverside dwelling units.

A neat triangle of lighted windows denoted Mrs. Earnshaw's place among the trees. She was probably engaged in one of her interminable bridge evenings with the more wealthy of the private colonists. She herself was a wealthy woman living with a hired companion, and her unit was an Aladdin's cave of expensive imported furniture and knick-knacks. I had met her only once. I found her forbidding, with her mastiff countenance and foghorn voice; somehow she made me feel as though I had incorrectly trumped her ace. It was with regrettable pleasure that I remembered her unit was below the expected high-water mark. . . .

I throttled the motor back and eased *Carousel* carefully up the dim creek; it wouldn't do to miss the channel and run aground. With the ebbing tide, we would have to wait until daybreak before we could get off again. Which would mean wading home across the creek, leaving the boat abandoned and listing. I could imagine the lash of Jane's tongue as she struggled through the stinking, knee-deep mud . . .

"Who shall I fall in love with, Jane?" I asked lightly, playing along.

She laughed, and the awkward moment was past. "Not with me, anyway. When I get married, it'll be to a man, not a love-sick drunken has-been."

"You'll be an old maid before you find the paragon you want, Jane. Remember what the Government says. It is the duty of the colonists to have children. Go forth and multiply."

"I'll multiply in my time, not the Government's, thanks. I'm only nineteen; there's ages yet. You're thirty or more—I reckoned you were too old even for Sheila. And the way you live you'll be sterile in ten years, if the blackfish don't get you first."

Now I was laughing too; there is something refreshing about Jane. "How are you getting on with young Phipps?" I asked. "You two seemed to be enjoying yourselves in the Club the other night."

"He's gorgeous," she replied briefly, shuddering with simu-lated ecstasy. Then she jumped to her feet, seized the boathook and went forward to pick up the mooring. "We're there," she called, swinging with one hand from the forestay while she reached across the water with the hook. "Throttle her back, father-figure. Reverse! Got it . . ."

I obeyed, and there was a rattle as she dragged the mooring chain to the deck and made it fast, mumbling with disgust as her hands became coated with greasy black slime from the river bed. We climbed into the dinghy and rowed for the timber jetty, where the single naked lamp glowed from a pillar. We had left it late; the tide was almost out and I had to skate the rowboat over the last few feet, pulling hard on the oars and forcing the grounded keel over the sloppy mud. We disembarked and I made the painter fast.

"Coming for a drink, Jane?" I asked. The lights of the colony rose up the hillside before us; bright against the skyline the windows of the Research Station and the Social Club beckoned. I saw the Reverend Blood flitting past in his black robes like some nocturnal bird of prey.

"No, thanks. I can leave it alone when I want to. In any case, it's not because of me personally that you offered. You just want to be seen in there with a young piece. Boosts your flagging ego."

"True," I admitted, chuckling. The jetty was wet and slippery; the lower road was covered with mud left behind from the previous high tide. I wondered just how far the water would reach at its peak in two weeks' time, and hoped that one hundred feet was a generous estimate. Vaguely perturbed, I took Jane's arm and piloted her up the hill beyond the last tide mark. We stood and looked down at the creek. It must have been fifty feet below us, at least.

"You can let me go now, you dirty old man." She detached herself. "Seriously though, Mark. Do you think its a good idea to spend every evening in the Club? Why not go home and have a cup of coffee, and sit down and read or something." In the light from a window I caught her smile as the stultifying aspect of the suggestion struck her. "I'll bring Alan over later, and we'll all have dinner together."

"Thanks for the invitation, Jane," I replied sarcastically, "but I've got better things to do than playing gooseberry to a young couple in love."

"In what? Don't get any wrong ideas about me and Alan. It's just sex, that's all." She laughed. "Suit yourself, then . . . See you tomorrow, I expect." She walked quickly away and the street was suddenly quiet.

I began to climb the hill. Now that the promise of a drink was imminent I began to think what lay behind it. Sitting in the bright clubroom with a glass in my hand, occasionally talking shop with my colleagues but more often listening to the conversation of the private colonists, interjecting the odd remark in the hope of steering the talk in the one direction everyone had avoided for the last six months. Feeling the frustration because they wouldn't talk about it, because they thought *I* didn't want to talk about it. . . .

They were considerate; they thought it would hurt me to talk about Sheila. But without a free, general discussion, I would never be able to clear the air. I would always be looked upon with pity, as the man whose future wife had been found dead, three days before the wedding. I wanted them to forget that.

Riverside is a small colony. Everyone knows everyone else. People gossip, they tell tales and speculate, and occasionally a surprising truth will emerge from a hint in casual conversation.

Such as who killed Sheila.

TWO

Sunday noon

The Social Club was crowded as ever with colonists downing appetizers before lunch and the air was thick with tobacco smoke and varied accents. The interior of the place is exceptionally comfortable—this may be due to the fact that John, the steward, is a relative newcomer, having arrived from Earth a few years ago full of ideas of what a bar ought to look like.

He is on the payroll of the Station and receives a flat salary without commission on sales, but this has not affected his willingness to make the place go. It is largely due to John's efforts that the private colonists of Riverside now look on the club as being as much their own meeting place as that of the Research Station—which has worked wonders for public relations. In view of this, I have never balked at John's frequent requisitions for new equipment, and the original clinical plastic furniture (Government Issue) has now all been replaced by comfortably upholstered items from the new factory in Oldhaven.

His final touch, which provoked opposition from the local puritans, was to replace the original sign, which had read: "LIQUOR. Persons under the age of fourteen prohibited. Music and dancing prohibited," with a board carrying an accurate representation of a Riverside trawler and the legend: "Welcome to the Riverside Social Club." He is a popular steward and on good terms with our single policeman, the unambitious Officer Clarke.

I shouldered my way to the bar and ordered a beer, drank deeply, and relaxed with my back against the counter, surveying the room. Most of the regular customers were present, the Station employees mingling with the private colonists in satisfactory manner. I was surprised to see Arthur Jenkins, the psychiatrist, in evidence together with another member of his team, Don McCabe, a red-headed man with a peculiar accent, recently out from Earth. They sat with their backs to the window, talking quietly; behind them the domed roofs of the colony fell steeply to the waterline. It was high tide and the water must have been over sixty feet above the mean sea level; the lower colony had a deserted look. Farther down, a few domes projected above the surface like capsized boats. I assumed that Arthur and Don were observing us, waiting for us to go berserk or whatever. As far as I was concerned they were wasting their time. I had a slight hangover; I lacked the enthusiasm to go berserk.

I found myself wheeling around like an ill-tempered dog as someone clapped me on the shoulder and bellowed a greeting in my ear. It was Paul Blake, twenty, single, opinionated and, this morning, utterly unbearable. I snarled and turned away.

"Not feeling too good this morning, Professor Swindon?" John Talbot was leaning across the bar, murmuring sympathetically in my ear.

"Very frail," I admitted.

"Big night last night," John observed. "But you won through in the end."

It had been a struggle. It is one thing to get Government permission to requisition trawlers but a different matter to implement the order and persuade the fishermen to move out to sea tomorrow. Which meant today. I noticed several of the fishermen in the club, drinking steadily. The afternoon's trip down river could be stormy. Farmer Blackstone was with them, drinking large scotches and posing another of the little conundrums that make Riverside interesting. He farmed the least economical spread in the area and was well known for failing to meet his quotas—his Arcows were scraggy and often appeared underfed—yet he was never short of cash. How did he afford his rate of living? Nobody knew—least of all, I suspect, the tax authorities.

"You'll feel better after a beer or two," John continued. "There's nothing like a beer at noon to sink a hangover . . . One thing, though," his voice became mock-serious. "It's fatal to over-correct."

"Don't worry," I reassured him. "I've got to keep a clear head for the afternoon."

I took my glass and walked over to where Jane and Alan Phipps were chatting with a group of fishermen. It's good policy to be seen chatting with the private residents as much as possible—and it makes a change of conversation, too. Our dynamic young scientists at the Station talk fish, think fish and —I've seen it myself—eat fish. The exceptions are the few members of the Agricultural Division, whose existence circles like a satellite around the Arcow, Arcadia's meaty herbivore. My department is marine, but I find that I have learned quite enough about the Arcow, too.

Jane greeted me effusively and invited me to sit beside her, but the reaction of the others was mixed. Conversation ran down like a burned-out armature.

"We were just talking about all the fish in the creek," said Jane brightly.

"It's not natural," muttered Eric Phipps, Alan's father, gloomily.

"I should have thought it was just what you wanted," I said.

"Too many. A glut. Lowers the market. In any case, you've stolen our boats. And they're mostly blackfish, anyway."

"Look," I said patiently. "I only need your boats for two or three weeks, and you'll be compensated for that. And with all these plankton, the estuary will be alive with fatties when the tide gets back to normal. The blackfish won't stay. They're rare in these waters. I can't think why they're here now."

Eric Phipps chewed at his cigarette; the end was damp and ragged. I never like to use the same ashtray as him. "Something to do with the Research Station, I'll bet . . . The Phipps' have fished this estuary for a hundred years, ever since Riverside was founded," he grumbled. "Never had our boats taken away from us before."

He was a man of medium height and nondescript appearance which belied his fervour when aroused. I have known my younger scientists to poke fun at him in the Club; with his slight alcoholic tremor and vacant face, he looks the archetypal moronic village yokel. I have seen him turn the tables on these occasions, leaping to his feet with surprising agility for his age and confronting those whose insults had become too much, his bleating ferocity putting me in mind of a mad sheep. His personality would have changed in an instant, and his opponents would find that the entire club had become uncomfortably hostile . . . At present, however, he was merely depressed.

"You'd be about sixty-five, Eric," I guessed. "Did your father ever tell you what happened during the last time of the high tides? Do you remember anything about it?"

He hesitated. "My dad died," he said at last. "It seemed there was some sort of fight on the boat. He had a mate whom he didn't get on with well. But it was never that bad, so they say. One of the hands saw it all. This mate just stuck a marline spike into Dad—without any reason, so it seemed."

"Had there been any quarrel that day, do you know?"

"Not that you'd take any notice of. My dad did say some day he'd get Wharton—that was the mate—but it was only talk. He often used to say that because it was Wharton who caused him to lose his hand, through stupidness with the winch. I was young then. I'm sure he never meant it, though."

Jane broke in. "For heaven's sake, Mark, let's talk about something different. What's the latest news on the tides?"

"They still say a hundred feet maximum. That'll be in something over a week. The cycle takes around twenty hours, so you'll have your moons back in due course—all of them. That should be quite a sight." I was calculating; the Arcadian day lasts twenty-six standard hours. "We'll be getting the low tides in daylight before long."

Alan Phipps spoke slowly. "The estuary will dry right out, apart from the narrow channel and a few pools. They'll be thick with plankton—and fish."

Now there's something I don't much like. Young Phipps is known to be a poacher. His methods are crude. He bombs the fish and collects them as they drift, stunned, to the surface. One day he'll be caught, maybe by his own father . . . He is a tall good-looking lad with dark hair and a pleasant, slightly dare-devil manner which the girls find attractive. Something of a lone wolf, he is rarely to be seen in the company of the other young men; Tom Minty, for instance, leaves him well alone. My own impression is that he combs his hair too much. I hoped Jane wasn't getting in too deep with him. . . .

"Mark?"

I looked up. Arthur Jenkins was standing by my chair. I excused myself and followed him over to the bar. The crowd by this time was beginning to thin out.

"I'd like you to do something for me," he began without preamble. "You must have guessed that we're here to keep an eye on things during the tides, in view of what happened last time. Now, you've got a boat and you're more in contact with the private residents than anyone else in the Station. I'd like you to keep me posted. Let me know anything that happens. Anything that might strike you as odd, in the next week or so. I can't go out on the boats—you know how the fishermen resent any sort of intrusion, and if they thought I was spying on them there would be hell to pay. But you can do this for me."

"Why watch the boats, particularly?" I asked.

"Whatever happened fifty years ago was connected with the water. It only affected the coastal colonies. There were inquiries at the time of course; but the odd thing was, nobody seemed to know what went wrong. Either they knew nothing and couldn't understand what had happened to people, or else, in the case of those tried for murder and assault, they said vaguely that they had to get the victim before he got them—not much of a defence. There was a mass mutual antipathy, which in many cases turned to violence. Also, the victims—those who lived—didn't seem to know *why* they were attacked. And they say there were a lot of suicidal drownings . . ."

"You realize I'm taking all the boats out to the point this afternoon? They won't be based on the colony for the next few weeks."

"That's all right. You watch the fishermen, I'll watch the rest. But be careful. Don't ask too many questions. Just watch."

He needn't have warned me. I knew the attitude of the private residents toward strangers and those who appeared over-inquisitive; the Riverside people would be secretive and insular. And I had been watching for six months already. . . .

The tide was ebbing as the eight trawlers swept down the estuary on the strong current. I had left *Carousel* anchored at the point and now stood with Perce Walters in the tiny wheelhouse of the leading boat. Perce was one of the more tractable of the trawler skippers, a powerful man of forty. During last night's discussion at the club he had shown common sense and helped considerably to talk the others around.

The remaining trawlers were strung out in line astern. From time to time I glanced around to reassure myself that everything was in order, but I needn't have worried. The boats were in capable hands. Nevertheless I wouldn't have put it past Eric Phipps, for example, to run his boat onto the rocky shore as we were passing Anchor Pool and claim compensation from the Government, saying that he would never voluntarily have taken the boat out in so strong a current.

"That's where Sheila was found drowned. The back of her head was stove in."

The remark hit me like a jolt of high voltage. "That's right," I said, recovering quickly. Maybe, at last, someone wanted to talk about it.

"What?" Perce was looking at me in vague puzzlement.

"She was in the water among those tree roots," I said. "The police said she must have fallen in and hit her head."

"That's what they said," confirmed Perce. "Look, Professor. I'm sorry. No offence. I must have been thinking aloud. I often do that. I know you don't want to talk about it. I wouldn't upset you for the world."

"That's O.K., Perce. I'm not upset. It happened six months ago; things begin to look better after a while. I'd rather talk about it than have everyone avoiding the subject and pitying me."

"That makes sense. But when you started to . . . spend each night in the club, well, we all felt you were drowning your sorrows. We sometimes talked about it while you were out, but there seemed to be an agreement that we never spoke of it while you were there."

"I suppose that would happen," I admitted. I decided to go straight to the point. "What do *you* think about Sheila's death, Perce?"

He flinched. I think it was the word "death" that did it. Over the years a strange politeness, a circumlocution almost, has developed in Riverside; the colony is pretty remote, and contact with the outside world is infrequent except through the medium of the Station and the weekly fish trucks. They don't use words like "death"—such language is coarse. If they want to say something unpleasant, they tend to conceal it in the jam of euphemism.

"As the police said, it was bad luck," he muttered.

I realized something else. In all probability they had discussed Sheila's death very seldom. In five years I had learned something of the Riverside attitude, but there was still a lot I didn't know. From what I had gathered about the outlook of the sub-colony as a whole, however, a sudden death would be avoided as a topic of conversation. It held the stigma of disgrace. One of the clan, any one of them, could be a killer.

Arcadia is almost aggressively decentralized; the Government is acknowledged only grudgingly by the scattered settlements. In Riverside they look to the Colony Committee for a lead, rather than the Arcadian Council. No doubt this would be one of the reasons for the scarcity of information concerning the previous time of high tides; the bereaved coastal colonies would have resented Government investigators prowling around. . . .

All speculation was driven from my mind as the trawlers raced between the headlands and out of the estuary with appalling speed. Perce was wrestling with the wheel, and I caught a reproachful glance from him—he would never have made this trip of his own free will. The sea approach to the river is littered with jagged rocks. They are not buoyed; many of them lurk inches below the surface and the fishermen avoid them from memory.

At this time the water level was average but the current was doubly swift and course corrections had to be made early. Now was the time when I had to place reliance on the men at the helms. Now, any impecunious and embittered fisherman might take the opportunity to wreck his ship. I scrutinized the speeding line of trawlers astern with anxiety. . . .

But I had reckoned without the fierce pride of these men. The line held, snaking among the unseen obstructions, which at this speed could rip the bottom straight out of a wooden hull. None of those eight men intended to be the one who, by a slight mistake, laid his seamanship open to question. At one point, as the file passed beyond the tall headlands, my stomach lurched as the trawlers scattered in all directions like worried sheep; but the formation was soon resumed, and I realized that each skipper had his own idea as to the safest passage at that point and would follow his own experience rather than trust to Perce's leadership.

"Made it all right, Professor." Perce was grinning at me, an unexpected show of emotion on his broad face. I think he had been as anxious as me. . . .

Relaxing, I watched the huge shape of a scoopbill winging in from the sea. It fed on the wing, its sinuous neck hanging low and its shovel beak skimming plankton from the surface. As it changed course to avoid us there was a surprising moment of drama. A blackfish leaped from the water, seized the bird by the neck and dragged it thrashing and flapping to the surface. A fierce battle ensued before the scoopbill tore its self free and rose, screaming with fear and pain, wheeled and headed out to sea again. It was a formidable bird, with powerful talons and a wing span of at least twelve feet—I had never known a blackfish attempt to take one before. I glanced at Perce; he raised his eyebrows and shrugged. "They're taking mewlers as well," he said. "They seem to be acting queer, lately."

We veered to port in a wide arc, the water becoming calmer all the time; our headlong pace slackened. The surface was littered with flotsam scoured from the estuary. I noticed a mattress and part of a chair—despite all the warnings, someone had left their evacuation too late . . . Then we reached the anchorage and Perce killed the engine. The anchor splashed, the chain roared out, checked, and we were safely moored.

I watched the other boats drifting to rest. We were positioned beneath the tall cliffs about a mile from the mouth of the estuary. I looked up and saw the slender tripod of the portable crane projecting into the sky like a lonely sentinel. Then a group of figures appeared at the clifftop. I saw Jane wave. They had been watching our passage between the headlands.

The next hour was spent in loading the sacks of fodder into the trawlers. I was surprised at how quickly it was done. The skippers seemed to have entered into the spirit of the thing. Perhaps the operation was now being regarded as a challenge to their seamanship. The team at the top had already lowered a number of sacks to the narrow shingle beach at the cliff base, and we transported these to the trawlers by means of a large dinghy I had requisitioned for the purpose. Before long the winches were grinding and the anchors emerged dripping from the water. Soon we were under way again, making for the pens. I was delighted, exchanging jokes with Perce in my pleasure at how smoothly the operation was going. Of course, it would be different later in the month, when we would be working at night. . . .

We had sixteen pens, and eight trawlers to deal with them. Perce and I took the farthest two. I had allowed for the water being opaque with suspended mud from the estuary and had tied floats at each corner of the pens, on long ropes. These buoys now dotted the surface of the sea and we moved through them slowly as the other boats, one by one, drifted to rest and began to jettison the food. Eventually we reached our own position and Perce throttled back, and my elation subsided. . . .

The sea was littered with dead, floating fish.

"There's a blackfish loose in the pen," Perce observed heavily.

I was already pulling on the diving gear.

"You're not going down?" he queried sharply. "Don't be a damned fool, Professor. The water's dirty. You won't see a thing, but the blackfish will smell you."

"That's what I'm hoping," I said. "That's how I'm going to get him."

I didn't allow him any further time for protest. I jumped overboard, grabbed a dead fatty and rubbed it roughly over my body, and sank. My last sight was Perce's concerned face peering over the gunwale; then the faceplate of the mask went opaque brown, darkening rapidly as I descended through the chill water. . . .

I am a natural coward. I excuse myself from this shortcoming by telling myself that cowardice is the product of a sensible, logical imagination. Only fools are brave. If anything unpleasant has to be done—and in the field of marine biology this occurs often—I therefore try to act without thinking, immediately.

As the water became near-black I was regretting the impulse; but that was what I had expected. It was too late now. Occasionally a dark shape would appear before me and my heart would lurch and I would tighten my grip on the knife, but the harmless fatty would move off with a lazy flick of its tail and I would be alone again, waiting to be attacked. I was banking everything on the fact that blackfish are rare in these waters, that the sudden proliferation in the estuary was a localized phenomenon due in some way to the excess of plankton. This despite the fact that I knew blackfish did not feed on plankton. . . .

If there was a shoal of blackfish in the pen I might just as well rip off my mask and drown; it would be less painful. . . .

THREE

I don't know what I was expecting; I suppose I imagined that the brute would become visible as a blurred outline waiting at the limit of visibility, sizing me up before making a swift frontal attack. It would go for my left arm as I held it outstretched; it would roll on its back as it struck, and I would jerk my arm away, jamming the knife into the white belly with my right hand. . . .

The sudden jolt in my upper calf caught me completely by surprise, back-somersaulting my body through the water and disorienting me utterly. There was no immediate pain; it was more like a heavy, accidental collision. It wasn't until I saw the streaming arc of dark blood trailing from my leg that I realized that the collision was real. The massive streamlined shape of the blackfish wheeled in an instant. I curled myself into a tight ball as it shot past, rolling and exposing an open trap of needle teeth, a long silver belly . . . I missed with the knife; I was too late, off balance. The brute looked huge in the submarine magnification; even allowing for that, it must have been eight feet long.

It was behind me. I twisted frantically, flinching in anticipation of the tearing jolt, which had been known to rip away a thigh. I saw it coming, realized that we were drifting towards the surface—the paler water was turning scarlet with my blood. It went for the leg again. This time the knife jerked in my hand and I saw the thin slit lengthen along its belly as it passed. I rolled to face it.

The next time it came slowly, almost thoughtfully, the jaw hinging open and shut as it prepared for the final thrust, the downturned mouth sad as though it had tasted something unpleasant. A wraith of blood drifted around it; my cut must have gone deep. . . .

22

I was not the only coward in that fishpen. The blackfish drove forward, jaws agape, rolling, and at the last moment the dim brain behind those tiny eyes must have recalled a previous pain. It swerved away, close to my waist, and this time I plunged the knife home, ripping open the full length of the belly, exposing a twisted mass of entrails which hung as the brute continued to roll, streaming behind as the blackfish went into a frenzied paroxysm of death, looping through the water, snapping at its own guts. I found that I was screaming into my mask. . . .

I was on the surface. Hands were grasping my shoulder, my armpits. A pain in the ribs as I was dragged over the gunwale. Flat on the deck, I opened my eyes and looked into the friendly, concerned face of Perce.

"You all right?" he asked.

I opened my mouth, tried to speak, failed. My voice had gone. I must have been screaming continuously for the past few minutes. Ashamed, I nodded weakly.

Jane had insisted on being lowered down the cliff face in order to accompany me home in *Carousel*. The rough bandages carried on board the trawlers smelled of diesel, and Perce seemed to think I ought to get to a doctor as soon as possible. Already the tide was fairly low, too low for the larger boats. The only alternative to *Carousel* was a bumpy ride behind the hovertruck along the path from the point, after having been winched up the cliff. I couldn't face that.

Perce came with us and the other fishermen went up the cliff, grumbling at having to leave their boats in an exposed anchorage. While Perce steered and the little outboard roared flat out against the current, Jane saw to my leg, insisting that I lie still. She had obtained some clean dressings from *Carousel's* cabin, and she peeled away Perce's crude attempts at bandaging, muttering to herself in the way that women do when confronted with a man's work in a woman's field.

Then she transferred her irritation from Perce to me. "That was a damned stupid thing to do, Mark," she said. "You could have been killed. All for the sake of a few fatties."

Perce was grinning down at me from his seat at the tiller. "He had no choice," he said. "The blackfish would have killed every fatty in the pen, and then moved on to the next."

Jane, having got the original bandages off, was exclaiming at the deep wound in my calf. "You're going to need stitches in this," she remarked with an odd sharpness in her voice. Her hand was trembling against my leg, and I wondered if perhaps she was a little more squeamish than she tried to appear. "You're going to be laid up for a few days. It's gone right through the muscle. Christ, Mark, don't you think your work's more important than a fatty or two?"

I expected that, but her next remark caught me completely off balance.

"Because, my darling, what would I do if you got yourself killed? What would there be left for me?"

I stared at her. "What did you say?" I asked, stupefied.

"I said don't you think your work's more important than a few damned fish," she replied waspishly.

"I mean after that; didn't you say . . . ? I mean, I thought you called me . . ." I couldn't repeat it; it was too ridiculous.

The loss of blood was making me light-headed, I thought.

To be sent to bed on doctor's orders is one of the great pleasures. A token struggle is put up, of course. The dialogue follows a rigid pattern. The patient's feeble protests—he has a lot of work to do, his illness or injury is slight, he feels better already—are countered by the doctor's dire, half-joking threats of amputation or pneumonia, as the case may be. Then the physician departs, his duty done; and the patient relaxes with the feeling that he has put one over on the expert and has successfully shed all responsibilities for the next few days. The doctor who habitually orders his patients to bed will retire a wealthy and popular man.

It is a sad reflection on human nature that boredom soon sets in and the invalid becomes querulous and ungrateful for the attention received from his voluntary nurses. By three o'clock on the following afternoon I had indulged in a vicious row with old Annie, Perce Walters' mother, because she was slow with the beer when I hammered the broom handle on the floor for attention. She is slightly deaf, and in various ways a little strange. During the brief time she looked after me she appeared nervous, as though she had read somewhere that bedridden men are prone to uncontrollable bouts of sexual excitement. She never came near me, passing me a glass of beer at arm's length, then backing off rapidly before, presumably, I could have my way with her. She must be seventy.

She left my service six hours after taking up her temporary unpaid position; her parting shot—for which I didn't much care —was that she would send Jane along to deal with me. Jane, she informed me, wouldn't stand for such nonsense. Jane would send me straight to the Station sick bay, where they had nurses who were paid to put up with such tantrums.

Jane, heedless of the doctor's advice, my own weak objections, and the supposed peril of sexual attack, had me out of bed within ten minutes of her arrival, downstairs in a dressing gown and an easy chair within arm's reach of the refrigerator. She put a stool under my foot, I'll say that much for her. She then changed my dressings, bending low over my leg so that I could see down her dress as far as the navel, caught my eye as she straightened up, told me that excitement was bad for a person who had lost blood, further informed me that she was not prepared to risk her reputation by staying in the unit with a dirty old man like me, and left, laughing in unseemly fashion considering my state of health. She said she would be back later in the evening and until then I could look after myself. I recalled that in her short stay she had called me a dirty old man on three occasions. It was becoming a fixation with her.

I lay back in my chair and tried to analyse my feeling of mild disappointment that she had gone, and my thoughts returned to the extraordinary hallucination I had experienced in the boat the previous evening. The remark I had thought I heard almost paraphrased something Sheila had said to me over a year ago, after I had been diving to repair a break in one of the pens. The job had taken longer than I had expected, and when at length I surfaced, Sheila was staring down at me from the cockpit of *Carousel*, her long hair hanging towards me; there were tears in her eyes. I climbed into the boat and held her close, but she was trembling for a long time. . . .

Sheila would have made the imagined remark; Jane, never. Much sought after by both my younger colleagues and the resident youths, Jane was a popular figure in the colony, always enjoying herself, with apparently little thought for the future. In the Club she always gave as good as she got; her language, on occasion, could be surprising. Yet despite all appearances to the contrary, I had a shrewd suspicion that she was a virgin. . . .

My deliberations were cut short by a knock at the door. I shouted that it was unlocked and Arthur Jenkins entered, looking clumsy and ill-at-ease, like a hospital visitor. And like any patient, my eyes dropped to his hands to see what he had brought. It was a wrapped bottle.

"Brandy," he informed me, removing the paper and setting the bottle on the table beside me. "Where do you keep the glasses?" It appeared that the brandy was not intended for me alone.

I indicated the cupboard and he found two small mugs, looked at them doubtfully, then filled them and sat beside me. "How are you feeling?" he asked.

We exchanged the usual awkward remarks and fell silent. He gazed at the ceiling while I regarded my leg. At last he cleared his throat and spoke again.

"Ah, Mark. This accident of yours. I haven't heard the full story yet."

So I explained exactly what had happened and he listened intently, looking at his hands as though he regretted not having brought a notebook.

"And would you have done that sort of thing under normal circumstances?" he asked when I had finished.

"They were normal circumstances."

He looked surprised. "You mean you make a habit of diving in among blackfish?"

I saw what he was getting at. "This has nothing to do with your phenomenon," I assured him. "I've had blackfish get in before; the pens are only fine nylon net, weighted and anchored at the bottom, with hollow bar floats at the top. Occasionally a blackfish will tear the net and get in. Usually there's no problem —the water's clear and I can take the speargun and kill at long range. No. If you're hoping the moons had driven me crazy, you're wasting your time."

"Oh." He was disappointed. "Nevertheless, something is happening in the colony. We've had a couple of cases of unprovoked assault."

"I haven't heard of them."

"I suppose you're a bit cut off from things at present. They both happened last night. The steward of the club got beaten up on his way home, for one."

"John?" I was surprised. "I hope they catch the swine who did that."

"They have. In fact, he made no attempt to get away. He just stood there, putting the boot in, until they dragged him off."

"Who was it?"

"Will Jackson, the fisherman. Did he have a grudge against John, do you know?"

I pondered. "Not as far as I know. In fact, it's more the other way around. John detests Will, but he'd never let him know that. After all, Will's a good customer, and half John's job is to hide his feelings from people. When you're behind a bar, I reckon folks must get on your nerves pretty often, but John would never tell a person to his face . . . He told me once that Will reminded him of a hungry blackfish when he sees a young girl in the club. And the man's attitude is sort of arrogant, too; but John wouldn't let that get him down."

Will Jackson was one of the less likeable of the private colonists. He was middle-aged and thin but wiry, always wore a hat, and walked with a dignified upright stance which did not suit his baggy, frayed clothing. He sat in the same way, straight-backed as though his ribs were in plaster, and gossiped endlessly about the shortcomings of his fellow men and the desirability of young girls.

"The other case was strange too," Arthur said. "It appears that Paul Blake punched Janet Cox in the face, in the course of some lovers' quarrel on the bank of the estuary."

I chuckled. "There's nothing strange about that. Paul's a quick-tempered young bastard. Any girl goes with him at her own risk. They still go with him, though, because he's a good-looking lad and his father's worth a fortune." Ezra Blake runs one of the biggest agricultural holdings in the area.

"I've seen young Blake, and the girl too. Blake said just that—that the girl was after him for his money, and it annoyed him."

"She said she was pregnant or something?"

"No. She swears she didn't say anything. They were just standing there. He was talking about his dad's farm, of all things, and she was listening, when he suddenly lashed out at her."

"I expect she wasn't interested enough. She was bored and showed it because she wanted to get on with more immediate business, if I know Janet. He's a boastful lad, and her inattention must have irritated him. What does he say?"

Arthur hesitated. "He doesn't say anything much. I can't seem to get him to talk about it. He just says that he can't stand gold-diggers."

"Neither can I," I laughed. "She got what she deserved. You'll have to leave it at that. You're looking for mysteries, Arthur."

He poured another two drinks, thoughtfully. "Has it ever struck you how little we know about this planet of ours, Mark?" he asked. "We've been here one hundred and thirty years, and in that time it appears there's been so much work to do, so much effort in the business of merely keeping alive, making the place habitable and clearing ground and getting agriculture and industries going, that there's been very little time for research. When I arrived here I was amazed at the sketchiness of the records. We've found out nothing. Nothing. It's almost frightening." He would have made a good actor.

"I've found out plenty," I reminded him.

"In your own narrow field, I don't doubt that. Don't be insulted—my field is narrow too. And I've only been here a short while. I've found out less than you. My business is people's minds and their reactions to their environment—and I make the same mistake all the time. I keep applying Earth standards. Damn it, the Government called me straight from Earth to keep an eye on things during this phenomenon. What other standards can I apply? And now I can sense that things are beginning to go wrong, and I don't know what to do about it."

"It's lucky you haven't got an alien intelligence to deal with."

"Do you know, that was one of my big disappointments? Back on Earth, when they first told me about Arcadia, I thought maybe I'd get the chance to psychoanalyse some weirdie. Then I read the files, such as they are . . . Damn it, this place might be Earth in the Jurassic, except that there are so few predators. A good dinosaur in the back yard might have been interesting. But no. A few herbivorous mammals, birds, vegetation harmless apart from the stickers. Not one species of carnivorous animal. That's why it was chosen for colonization, I suppose. Nothing unusual except a bunch of people who run amok every fifty-two years."

"That ought to be unusual enough for you."

"But there's nothing to go on. It's like you suddenly punching me now, and saying you did it because you felt like it. Why did you feel like it? You can't answer. Or possibly you might say you hit me because you objected to my views. But why hit me *now*, when you've never done it before? Because all six of Arcadia's moons happen to be on one side of the planet? That doesn't make sense. God!" He made a gesture of despair which brought his hand dangerously near my bandages.

"Steady, Arthur." I shifted my leg. "If you go on like this you'll be the one who runs amok, with the colonists watching and cheering. Psychiatrist, analyse thyself. Why not just wait and see what happens?"

"I think it's started happening. How long do I wait for? Two hundred years, say? When we've got a coastal population of millions, all rioting every fifty-two years?"

Now, that was an unpleasant thought. I began to look forward to Jane and a breath of sanity. Then I recalled something he had said. There was not one species of carnivorous animal on Arcadia.

Until Man arrived. . . .

FOUR

Five days later I was walking unaided about the unit—stiffly, but nevertheless on my feet. This speedy recovery was due mainly to Jane's ruthless nursing. The girl seemed devoid of any womanly sympathy and more or less forced me to my feet with all the unthinking command of a sergeant-major. Not satisfied with that, she announced that the following day she would take me for a walk to get some fresh air into my lungs, as she put it. In vain I protested that my lungs were quite happy with their diet of cigarette smoke and that my pallid complexion was due to natural skin colouration allied to loss of blood. She would have none of it. She warned me to be up and ready for her the next day; otherwise she would withdraw her services like old Annie had, and leave me helpless and rotting.

During the days of my confinement I had heard a few reports of further disturbances in the colony. The crime wave was on the upswing. Arthur Jenkins dropped in several times looking increasingly worried; and Perce Walters told me about a fight in the Club of inexplicable origin, which had escalated like a bar-room brawl in one of those old-time Earth Westerns. Strangely, reports of these incidents always came from eye-witnesses or the victims; the aggressors were curiously reticent about the whole thing and unable to explain their actions.

I had been a little puzzled by an incident in my own unit. I don't know whether it had any connection with outside events, but it might well have. On the fourth day a salesman arrived. I admitted him grudgingly, thinking he was some sort of investigat-or—the colony is getting a complex about being watched—but it turned out he represented a new firm in Premier City that manufactured deodorant bottles—air fresheners, where you pull up a wick and pollute the atmosphere with a cloying scent. He sat and sniffed for a while before he revealed his business.

He had a pointed nose and a rat-like face; his sniff was convincing. I even began to sniff myself. Then he opened his case, and instead of bringing out the questionnaire I had expected, he produced a bottle with a wick. He set it on the table, close beside me. He stopped sniffing, looking relieved. I wonder that he didn't stop breathing altogether, with that stink. He then offered to sell me a dozen of the bottles, or a gross at reduced rates; he said a bottle would last three months and "dispel those unpleasant sickroom odours." It was highly concentrated, he assured me unnecessarily. They used large quantities at the Social Club, and he had been recommended to call on me by a red-haired young lady he had met at the bar. I struggled to my feet in some annoyance.

He bleated something about the economics of the gross pack (thirty-six years' supply, I calculated), then he stopped dead, staring at me, his eyes dilating. He was not a big man—I overtopped him by several inches. I watched in astonishment as his face paled, his lips trembled, and he flung his forearm across his face as if to ward off a blow. Then he began to whimper—a thin, high-pitched sound. Wheeling around rapidly he dashed for the door, hunched as though expecting a bullet through the spine. I heard his feet pattering down the road; then there was silence. I sat down again, bewildered. His case was still on the table. Jane took it back to him later.

Jane arrived after lunch, sensibly clad in slacks and pullover, thick shoes, and an aroma of gin and tonic—a girl prepared for healthy exercise. I was ready, and we set off down the hill towards the small bridge that spans the head of the creek. My painful limp appeared to amuse her; she kept grinning at me and soon took my arm, calling me Grandpa, which was a change from her normal mode of address but no more flattering.

In the few days I had been out of circulation the tides had moved around, and the bridge was uncovered though muddy. A nearby clump of dagger trees looked bedraggled; the lower branches and spines were slimy and festooned with weed and flotsam. The dwelling units in the immediate area presented a decayed appearance, and I wondered how long it would take to make them habitable again once the spring tides had ceased. It would take weeks to dry them out and they would all require

repainting, which would be a costly business, although we had
been assured there would be compensation coming. I only
hoped the Government kept their word. Like Governments
throughout the colonized Galaxy, the Arcadian Council was not
renowned for keeping promises made in times of emergency.

Once over the bridge we began to climb again, bearing right
and taking the track which eventually reaches the point. I
didn't think I could walk that far, although I would like to have
been able to reassure myself that the fish-feeding operation had
been going smoothly in my absence. Perce Walters had been
deputizing for me and had reported back daily that everything
was in order. I hoped he was right. He was a good man, but I felt
he would say anything to assure my peace of mind.

The track crosses a meadow for the first quarter-mile past the
bridge. There are one or two scattered units here, owned by
people who like to be away from the bustle of the colony across
the creek. The units were deserted now, the owners having been
forced to move, with much grumbling, to temporary lodgings in
the upper colony. Gratitude is not a characteristic of refugees.

Beyond the meadow the afforested area commences, stretch-
ing all the way to the point. The trees are similar to monkey-
puzzles, with here and there a group of ancient conifers and other
even more primitive trees—the half-plant, half-bush known as
the sticker. There branches, or tentacles, are prehensile to a
degree, and although their chief diet is butterflies, kite-bugs and
other flying or ground insects, they have been known to take
worrals. There are legends told by Jed Spark of them taking
small children, but this I doubt. Certainly there has been no
recorded instance in my time.

Thinking of worrals reminded me of Alan Phipps. I asked
Jane how the romance was progressing.

"He wants us to get engaged," she replied. "We were in the
club this morning celebrating."

"Congratulations."

"Premature, Grandpa. I didn't say yes. We were there, and it
seemed as good a reason as any to celebrate. The time, the place,
and the boy. Your mind runs along channels as undeviating as
the bed of the creek. And just about as dirty too," she added
gratuitously. "You don't have to have a purpose for a celebra-
tion."

"Oh." I thought that one over. "Well, I hope that in due course you will be very happy," I said formally.

"You'll be losing a daughter-figure. How does that grab you?"

"I never was one for responsibilities. I suppose he's promised you a worral coat for a present."

"My suggestion, actually. It delays things. It takes a long time to match the pelts up, and he'll have to trap a hell of a lot of—" She broke off, gazing at me in dismay. "You crooked bastard, Mark," she said.

"Now look here, Jane," I said seriously. "The worral is a protected animal. I've had a suspicion for a long time that young Phipps is trapping them. What with bombing the fish and trapping the animals he'll denude the area of wildlife before long. And if Mrs. Earnshaw catches him . . ."

Mrs. Earnshaw is President of the Riverside Society for the Preservation of Our Dumb Friends. By no means dumb herself, she indulges in a series of bitterly-fought lawsuits on behalf of the Society and has, on occasions, succeeded in obtaining committals to prison for contravention of the Preservation of Wildlife Act. She is not generally liked. Nevertheless, I agreed with her principles.

"There's plenty of worrals," Jane muttered sullenly.

"There are now. Have you ever read about what happened on Earth? Centuries of indiscriminate hunting, trapping and poisoning; towns, roads and agriculture encroaching on wildlife; nobody bothering about the decreasing animal population until it was too late, and then salving their consciences by setting up reserves, or trying to breed tigers in zoos. But the ecology of the reserves was all wrong, and the tigers were too ashamed to breed in concrete pens in full view of the public, and they all died out. In the whole of Earth, there's only one wild species extant now."

"What's that?"

"The rat. It's protected, of course."

"Sorry, Pops. I'll have a word with Alan. I'll cancel the order.'

"He can always buy you a coat from one of the breeding farms."

"Expensive, and in any case I'm not sure I want one now."

"Perhaps you ought to take up with Paul Blake, then."

"I'm not that desperate."

Conversation seemed to die out, and I felt that any further remark by me would be rubbing it in. Fortunately, there was a diversion.

"Look!" exclaimed Jane.

The track followed the ridge to the point; we were in the huge rocky outcrop that fell steeply to Anchor Pool and the creek to our right. A few sparse trees clutched a precarious foothold on the granite. From a thick bough a worral was watching us with bright button eyes, peering over its furry shoulder as it clung to the tree with short forelimbs.

"They're lovely things," Jane murmured. "I wouldn't like to see them die out."   ,

"The trouble is, they're slow-moving and slow-breeding," I said. "They had no natural enemies until Man colonized Arcadia . . ." My gaze fell from the animal to the estuary below; Anchor Pool was framed by the spiky branches of the tree. The light was beginning to fail and the water looked cold and menacing, deep and mysterious beyond the tumbled boulders. Sheila and I used to walk along here; she would be chattering and swinging her ridiculous little yellow bag with the long strap; it would knock against her strong tempting legs as she walked, always getting in the way when we stopped to kiss . . . And when we kissed I would put my hands behind her neck and run my fingers through her long silky hair; and she would gasp, and hold me tighter; and she was found floating face down in the dark water of Anchor Pool, and the fine hair was dark with mud and thinly straggled about the terrible wound in the back of her head. . . .

"Mark. Don't."

"Sorry . . ." I relaxed consciously—Jane was watching me anxiously. "Maybe we shouldn't have come along here."

"You still don't believe it was an accident, do you?"

"I don't see how it could have been," I replied. "She would never fall—not from here. Why should she? The path's wide."

"Maybe she stumbled in the dark."

"What would she be doing along here in the dark? If only they'd been able to establish the . . . time of death . . ." I felt sick. They hadn't been able to establish the time of death because she had been in the water too long. . . .

Jane looked around desperately; I knew she wanted to change the subject. I was being unfair. It had been a very bad time for her, too. Sheila had been running the house for several years in her quietly competent way, ever since their parents had died in a boating accident. Jane had then been left completely alone.

Suddenly she pointed. "Look at the worral!" she exclaimed.

The little animal was bouncing up and down on the branch, displaying unusual agility. As I watched, it swarmed up the trunk, having apparently satisfied itself that it had captured our attention. It disappeared into a circular hole—a typical worral nest—then re-emerged backwards, dragging something. It was having some difficulty, and for a while it tugged at a kind of thong, squeaking with frustration. Suddenly the obstruction was cleared and the creature swarmed down the trunk to land with a small thud on the ground. It moved towards us warily, its eyes fixed on mine, dragging a bright object behind it.

Sheila's yellow handbag . . .

"God," I muttered. I strode forward and the worral retreated up the tree, resuming its perch. I bent and picked up the bag. My hands were shaking violently. I walked back to Jane; she was watching me wide-eyed.

"How. . . ?"

"I don't know. There's something funny going on here." I glanced around. In the darkening twilight the trees were menacing; their branches, moulded by the prevailing westerly winds, seemed to grasp for us greedily. Below, the estuary glowed with eerie phosphorescence, a broad ribbon of blue light blazing in an uncanny vortex at Anchor Pool, like a spiral nebula. I felt as though I was being drawn toward that pool of blue fire . . . A kite-bug drifted past; the fine net wrapped itself softly about my face and I started, clawing the phosphorescent gossamer away nervously.

"I'm scared, Mark. Let's get out of here." Jane's arms were around my waist and she was shivering against me as she gazed hypnotized at the estuary.

"You feel it too?"

And then suddenly I felt more than my own uneasiness. I felt Jane's trembling as though it were my own, and I began to shiver too, and cold white needles of fear probed my brain. My heart began to pound. I could hear Jane crying softly beside me as we both stared at the whirling pool of sapphire phosphorescence. . . .

Then I tore my eyes away, grasped Jane by the arm, and we stumbled back along the path to the village, our minds crying for haste but our feet dragging as though bound, while all the time Anchor Pool seemed to scream at us to stay and share its terror. . . .

Somehow we got back to the bridge, somehow we climbed the hill to my unit and fumbled the door open. We slammed it behind us, switched on the lights, and stood gazing at each other, blinking in the grateful brightness and normality of the familiar room. Jane sank into a chair, exhaling unsteadily, and I poured two large brandies. I sat down too and gradually became aware of the painful throbbing in my leg. I eased it onto a stool and loosened the bandages. Jane sipped her drink, gazing blankly before her.

At last I spoke. "Jane. . . ?"

"Yes?" She looked at me dully.

"Have you ever felt anything like that before? You've been along the track at night a few times, I expect." The path was notorious as a lovers' lane.

"Nothing like that ever happened."

"Tell me how you felt, just now."

Her face was pale with strain. "I felt scared," she said. "And I knew you were scared, and that made me more scared still. All the time the pool seemed to . . . draw me, sort of; and I felt terribly sad at the same time as being frightened. It was as though everything was finished . . . At the same time, as though something new and terrifying was starting. Something that was completely unknown. Completely strange. As though, somehow, I knew nothing about anything. As though, second by second, I was being born into an alien world. . . ."

It was as though everything was finished . . . My mind went back to her remark of several days ago. We had been talking about the disappearance of the last moon. Then she had said it was as though everything was finished . . . And I had thought her over-imaginative. I was not so sure now. I was not so sure that I trusted my own imagination. . . .

She was watching my face; she was hesitating as to what to

say.

"It was strong, that feeling of being pulled towards the pool," she said at last. "It was so powerful that I might not have been able to resist it, if I'd been alone."

"I felt it too."

There was a long silence before she said what we were both thinking. . . .

"Mark, do you suppose that's what happened to Sheila?"

FIVE

It is virtually impossible for the human animal to discipline its thoughts. A chance event will set up a sequence of notions which can race irresistibly, like a runaway train, to a horrifying conclusion. There is no going back from the conclusion once it is reached. It remains in the mind, scarring the memory's landscape with a wreckage of ideals. So it was after Jane left, and I tipped the contents of Sheila's bag onto the table.

I think we had both forgotten about the bag. Jane hadn't mentioned it since we reached my unit, and I had dropped it on the floor after entering. It was surprising that I still had it with me, after the panic flight from the pool.

The door closed behind Jane and I was alone, and gradually I became aware that I was looking at the bag. It lay on the carpet just inside the door. I picked it up, wondering whether I ought to call Jane back, but thought better of it. There was no point in harrowing her with the sight of Sheila's personal things. So I sat alone at the table regarding the pathetic heap of damp belongings; the word "effects" came unbidden into my mind. Sheila seemed very close at that moment.

The usual rubbish was there—lipstick, compact, comb, used tickets of various types, a few hair grips, one or two old letters, a small purse containing loose change. And a tight roll of thin clothing.

I opened it up. A man's nylon shirt and shorts, well worn . . .

It was like finding a gigolo in one's wife's bed. The objects were suggestively out of order in a sacred place. It was no good telling myself I didn't know what to think; my mind had already run ahead to an unbelievable conclusion, which I was only too ready to believe. To have someone else's shirt and shorts in your handbag denotes a certain easy familiarity with the person concerned. . . .

38

As I lay in bed my thoughts churned in increasing circles from the core of hard fact. The whole scene emerged: the opening, as Sheila and the man strolled, possibly hand in hand, along the track frequented by lovers. They would arrive at a suitable spot. He would rapidly undress; the ground would be damp and she would put his clothes in her bag. Preparing to undress herself, his nakedness would suddenly appeal to her sense of the ridiculous and she would decide to play hard to get. She would move away, laughing. He would follow and an erotic chase would ensue . . . My thoughts were strident with the sound of their laughter as they chased about the moonlit hillside. He had almost caught her. She twisted away and jumped to a granite boulder, stood there taunting him, swinging the bag as he grasped for her. Maybe he caught her by the ankles . . . Then she overbalanced and fell over the edge of the outcrop to tumble head over heels, smashing against boulders in her descent. They had found traces of blood on the rocks . . . The man climbed down, found her lying in the water, saw the wound on her head and took fright, searched for the bag for a few frantic moments without success, then crept naked back to the sleeping colony. . . .

There were loopholes in my theory, but I was tired, I had experienced a bad fright, and I was low enough to believe the worst. As I tried to get to sleep, the same indisputable facts kept recurring.

What other reason could Sheila have for walking along the track at night?

Why else should she have a man's possessions in her bag?

How else could she have fallen from a wide, safe path?

I was so sick with misery that I no longer blamed the unknown man. I wasn't looking for a murderer any longer—it was an accident. I fell asleep hating the memory of Sheila. . . .

I overslept, waking eventually with a foul taste in my mouth. I got up, dressed, made myself a cup of coffee, gathered up Sheila's things and tipped them back into the bag with the intention of taking it to the police. They would find it interesting and no doubt reopen the case.

Then I hesitated . . . I wasn't sure I wanted them to reopen the case. I didn't want to show the clothes to the police. I didn't want to admit they had come from Sheila's bag. I couldn't face the public sympathy and private ridicule which would follow the revelation that my girl had been knocking around with another man a few days before the wedding. . . .

Meanwhile, Jane knew I had the bag but she didn't know of the contents. All I had to do was hand the bag over to Officer Clarke and leave it at that for the time being. The business of the clothes could be let ride now that I, personally, was satisfied this was not a case of murder. I put the shirt and shorts in a drawer, snapped the bag shut and set off.

Rounding the corner at the foot of the hill, I found a large crowd gathered at the water's edge. Raised voices told me there was a dispute in progress. I hurried towards the gathering wondering if Arthur Jenkins had been correct—that this was the start of full-scale rioting. There was a tight knot in the pit of my stomach; I think events were getting the better of me. I was prepared to believe the worst of anything and everything.

Perce Walters saw me coming and called out. Heads turned and the heated discussion died. Despite their slight prejudice against the Station, the private colonists frequently look on me as an adviser on river matters. I think this is because of my knowledge of marine life; they respect a man who knows more than themselves in their own field. Jed Spark was there, leaning on his stick and frighteningly scarlet with unhealthy rage. I noticed his grandson Jim and two other young tearaways, Tom Minty and Bill Yong. Jane was there with Alan Phipps. Young Paul Blake observed reactions with superior amusement. Eric Phipps was in the centre of the group, which was gathered around a large truck containing two collapsed rubber dinghies and a roll of netting. There was, of course, no sign of Officer Clarke. Fortunately, none of my own people from the Station were there, either.

"What's going on here, Perce?" I asked.

He was staring at my hand. "That's Sheila's bag," he said slowly. "I'd recognize it anywhere."

Suddenly the attention of the entire group was riveted on the handbag. A thought flashed through my mind: The unknown man could be among the crowd. I examined their faces carefully. Surprise was there, and a kind of fear. The three youths—Minty, Spark, and Yong—were staring wide-eyed. It was easy to read guilt into each face, but it could have been superstitious dread or ghoulish fascination.

"I found it last night," I said. "There's nothing very interesting about it, but I thought I'd better take it to the police." I dismissed the matter. "What's going on?" I asked again.

Perce moved beside me and began to reason like a lawyer fighting a lost case. "I ask you, Professor," he said. "Is it right? Is it fair? We can't use our trawlers, you've taken them away from us—rightly so, too, considering the emergency," he added hastily. "We have to pay our river dues and licences to fish here. It's our living, and the law says you can't fish without a licence. We don't like that—we look on the river as our own property—but we pay our licences. Don't we, boys?"

A general murmur of assent.

"So you agree it's not right, Professor?"

"What's not right?" I asked. I seemed to have missed the point.

A large man in a stained shirt pushed his way through the crowd and stood before me, his fists on his hips, his expression belligerent. "You seem to be in charge here," he began, "so I'll tell you the facts. Then perhaps you'll tell this lot to get out of our way, and let us get on with our work."

"That depends on the facts." I didn't relish the position I found myself in. This man appeared sure of himself, but the private colonists were looking to me for support.

"We've come right from Inchtown."—(A cry of "and you can fucking well go right back there!")—"And we wouldn't come fifty miles unless we were sure of our rights. We've checked up. We don't need a licence for what we're going to do."

"What are you going to do?" I asked patiently.

"Trawl the creek for plankton. It's thick with plankton, like porridge. We'll get a good price from the factory at Inchtown. And you don't need a licence for plankton; normally it's not economic to bother with them. Fatties, you need a licence. Plankton, no."

He emphasized his points with a stubby forefinger against my chest. He was right.

"You'll get fatties in your net," I pointed out. "You'll be using a fine mesh; you'll pick up everything that swims."

He laughed shortly. "Fatties? With all the blackfish in the water? Not a chance . . . I tell you what I'll do. For every fatty I

catch, I'll give a donation of fifty Arcads to the church fund.
Fair enough?"

A suggestion of a church donation is always a winning
gambit; further objections seem churlish. "You'll need the cash
to pay the fine," I countered weakly. He took this as assent.

"That's it, then . . . George! Get the stuff off!" He walked
back to the truck amid a muttering from the opposition.

"You shouldn't have let him do it, Professor," protested
Perce.

"I'm sorry. There's nothing we can do. In any case, it doesn't
matter. The plankton's no use to us. Let's forget about it."

Nevertheless I was conscious that my stock had fallen. They
felt that I should have done something to stop the strangers.
Officer Clarke showed up a few minutes later and they began to
question him, rather than accept my opinion. His views bore me
out, but it made no difference. It was I who had given the
plankton-fishermen the go-ahead. I handed him Sheila's bag
and we moved along the street to watch the strangers set out.

They had a compressed-air cylinder, and within minutes the
two dinghies were inflated, the net loaded on board, the outboard motors clamped to the transoms. The bright yellow boats
roared off downstream.

"Another crisis averted, for the time being." A voice spoke
beside me.

"Oh, good morning, Arthur. Come to see the fun?"

Arthur Jenkins drew me aside. "That was a funny thing," he
observed quietly. "You noticed the set-up was ideal for a brawl.
Riverside thought its rights were being infringed. The foreigners
were riding roughshod over established custom. Yet it all went
off peacefully."

"Maybe it'll hot up when they get back."

"Possibly . . . I've been examining the reports of the various
incidents we've been having lately. We've had fifteen instances
of unexplained fighting so far."

"As many as that?" I stopped. The incident with the strangers
and the discovery in Sheila's bag had completely driven last
night's episode at the pool out of my mind. Hesitantly at first,
not wishing to appear an over-imaginative alarmist, I described
the events to Arthur.

He listened carefully. When I had finished he sucked at his

pipe, thinking.

"You described it as blue phosphorescence," he repeated slowly. "Whirling, with a hypnotic effect. Accompanied by a sensation of fear. Fear . . . Could fear drive people to attack each other? Not necessarily, I think. Let's consider this thing logically."

"Well," I ventured, "the phosphorescence was obviously billions of plankton rotating in the whirlpool effect caused by the swift outflow of tide through Anchor Pool. It was getting dark; the pool was the brightest object in view. Could it be that we just watched it for too long?"

"That might account for the hypnotism, but not necessarily the fear. You say you felt frightened because Jane felt the same, then the two of you seemed to get in the grip of some cumulative feedback?"

"That's right, and there was something . . . cosmic about it. As though we were . . ." I chuckled nervously, remembering my sensations of the previous night, which seemed ridiculous when described on the prosaic Riverside quay. "As though we were watching the creation of a spiral nebula." I hurried on. "The birth of something where no life had been before—something completely new . . . Do you know, when Jane and I were discussing it afterwards, we agreed that the sensation would have been difficult to resist for a person by himself . . . or herself. We even thought Sheila might have seen it and fallen down among the rocks as a result."

"Sheila? She was your fiancé, wasn't she? I heard about that. Tragic affair . . ." He looked awkwardly sympathetic.

"But she couldn't have seen it. She . . . died, six months ago."

"Besides which, you're not happy about the circumstances of her death," observed Arthur with uncanny insight. "Sorry, I shouldn't have said that. But it's obvious to me. I wonder how many other people think what you think . . . Was there any clue in the bag you found last night? I saw the effect it had on the local population."

"There was nothing interesting," I muttered.

He looked at me sharply. "Because if there was, I wouldn't try withholding it from the police. Make sure everything's in their hands before thay make the contents public. You know what a talker Clarke is. Otherwise, if we've got a killer in

Riverside, he might think you've kept something back for reasons of your own. And he might come looking for it. . . ."

I was saved from replying by a sudden buzz of comment from the watchers on the quay.

The two dinghies had strung the net between them and had started to move off, two men in each boat; they were about fifty yards downstream and seemed to be in difficulties. There were signs of commotion on the starboard craft. I saw a man jump to his feet, rocking dangerously. Cries of alarm reached us. The second dinghy cut loose from the net and veered to assist. The yellow fabric was subsiding, deflating; the crew leaped for the second dinghy, which wobbled, overloaded; then the motor roared and it headed back for the quay. I saw the fins of blackfish cutting the water. . . .

The blackfish, a huge shoal of them, swarmed between the dinghy and the quay, keeping pace with it, heading it off as it raced for safety. The fishermen were in confusion; I saw them pointing at the quay, urging the helmsman to make for land. The helmsman, however, had his eye on the fish and was keeping clear, knowing that once the dinghy ran among the shoal the thin fabric would be ripped to shreds. . . .

The boat was opposite us. Moving fast, it made for the bridge at the head of the creek, the blackfish keeping pace alongside. The helmsman, at last realizing he could not outrun the fish, put the tiller hard across and made full speed for the quay. . . .

It was over quickly. The fish were leaping into the boat, the men standing, fighting them off. Fish trailed from the yellow sides, tearing at the fabric. The men were screaming as the boat, out of control, veered in a tight circle, sank lower in the water, and spluttered to a halt as water entered the carburettor. They were about fifteen yards from the quay and there was nothing we could do to help. . . .

Later, Arthur invited himself up to my place.

He said: "I think we'd better put our heads together over this thing. I was watching those fish. They seemed to be . . . organized. . . ."

SIX

Like all Research Station dwellings, mine is of standard issue dome construction, two storeys high. As far as possible I have tried to create an atmosphere of informality; the inner walls are wood panelled, and locally made chairs and tables are scattered around the room in, to my mind, charming confusion. On the wall is a large bookcase, although the small occasional tables also bear their burden of reading material. It is pleasant to have everything at hand; I generally take my shoes off on entering—which economizes on time spent vacuuming the thick carpet—and I always know where to find them when I go out again.

Except when Jane is around. Jane likens the place to a pigsty and usually spends the first ten minutes of any visit concealing items of immediate use behind cupboard doors. She says she doesn't know what I would do without her to clear up after me. I know what I would do. I would find my shoes immediately on deciding to go out, instead of playing hunt-the-slipper among cupboards crammed full of old clothes and dismantled machinery getting fishhooks in my flesh.

It was the first time Arthur had visited the place. I opened the door and ushered him in, watching in some pride as he surveyed the room.

"This is a comfortable place you've got, Mark," he said. He sat down uninvited—a sure sign he felt at home—and filled his pipe. "No evidence of a woman's touch around here."

"Not yet," I said significantly. "But I think Jane will be along soon, once she's disposed of her boy-friend. She saw us leave the club together. She won't want to miss out on anything."

"Good," he said indistinctly from within a cloud of aromatic smoke. "I wanted to have a word with her, too. And then, if it's all right with you, I'd like you both to come down to Anchor

45

Pool with me."

Following the horrifying incident on the quay we had both recovered our nerve with a few much-needed drinks at the Social Club; and I decided it would be a good idea to have another right now, to consolidate things. As I was filling the glasses the door burst open and Jane came in fast and breathless. I introduced her to Arthur—they had scarcely met before, due to the latter's retiring habits—and she began to question him as to his views on the blackfish. I think his pipe lent him an air of knowledgeability.

"I've got an idea about it," he admitted. "Just a theory; maybe we'll know more after we've been down to the pool. But first, what do you know about the breeding habits of the plankton, Mark? I remember you had some pretty odd ideas when we discussed it at that lecture some time ago."

"I don't know any more now than I did then. I've kept them here in tanks, of course, under observation. But I've never seen them breed. They're unlike Earth plankton I've read about, in that they're remarkably long-lived and resistant to disease or changes in environment. I get the impression that the only time they die is when they're eaten by a fish, or meet with an accident. They're all the same species, each about three millimetres long and looking like a tiny shrimp. Or perhaps a lobster," I corrected myself, "because they've got miniature claws. I've never been able to observe that they grow any bigger. The lobsters we get outside the estuary mouth are similar to Earth lobsters, and their young, when hatched, look very much like these plankton. But that's the end of the similarity. The young lobsters grow fast and are susceptible to sudden changes in water temperature."

"So the plankton are pretty hardy little brutes."

"Oh, yes. They live forever."

Arthur tapped out his pipe and examined the bowl. "What would you say, Mark," he said slowly, "if I suggested that they have a life-expectancy of fifty-two years?"

I looked at him in amazement. "Fifty-two years? That's pushing it a bit. I know I said they lived forever, but I meant they live a long time considering their size. Nothing that small could live for fifty-two years."

"Some bacteria do."

"Yes, but that's different. The plankton are animal, with the metabolism which that implies."

"You've already established that there's something odd about their metabolism."

"Not *that* odd . . ." I began to think hard. In a way I was in a similar position to Arthur—in my research I was obliged to apply Earth standards until circumstances proved otherwise. They were the only standards we had; they were the standards we were taught at college. It was up to people like myself to investigate and revise these standards where necessary until a complete picture of Arcadian biology was built up. . . .

"Let's imagine the evolution of the plankton," Arthur went on. "Nobody ever knows what happened right in the beginning, but imagine that an extremely hardy strain of plankton somehow evolves. They spend their life drifting about the oceans— they can survive in extremes of temperature—and they are gradually consumed by fatties and other fish who prey on them. In order to continue the species, they must breed. And for some reason the ideal conditions only occur once every fifty-two years, at times of extreme tides.

"They make for the muddy estuaries. Maybe they are nourished by a particular type of mud which they can only reach at low tides; maybe some sort of photosynthesis is used which depends on the filtering effect of suspended particles in the water. Maybe it's a combination of both—I don't know. That's your province, not mine. Nevertheless, at the times of extreme tides they come to the estuaries to breed.

"This rare breeding is vitally important; if it ever failed, the species would die out. There would be no question of being able to exist for another fifty-two years and try again. The sea and the sky are full of predators, and I've no doubt the birth-rate, if you can call it that, allows only for an average number of deaths during one life-span.

"So during the breeding the plankton have to be protected, guarded every minute of the time. And what better guard than the ferocious blackfish, the killer of Arcadia's seas, which does not, however, prey on plankton. . . ? So a relationship is set up. For all I know it might be symbiotic—the plankton might perform some service at which I can't even guess. Anyway, somehow the blackfish are recruited as guards and, as we saw this morning, they perform their services conscientiously. . . ."

My glass was empty; I rose to pour refills all round. "An amazing theory, Arthur," I conceded. "Maybe you ought to have my job. For all I know, you may be right. It certainly explains the concentrations of blackfish."

"How do you explain what happened when Mark and I were looking at the pool?" Jane asked.

Arthur was ready for that one. "We don't know what sort of control the plankton exercise over the blackfish—always assuming that my theory is right. But just suppose its something transmitted instinctively, a sort of fear signal, like pigeons swerving simultaneously from an upraised gun, for instance. You might, at that moment, have caught the backlash of such a signal . . . Somehow at that moment you were attuned to it, and it affected you."

"Now we're getting into your field," I commented. "Can you relate this effect to the outbreaks of violence?"

"It's possible . . . Sudden irrational fear could, I suppose, cause a person to hit out."

"It won't do, Arthur," Jane said firmly. "And there's another point you've missed. Why is it that of all land animals only humans notice this effect? You'd at least expect the Arcattle to be restless, or start stampeding, but nobody's reported that. In any case, fear doesn't explain half the sensations we had."

"The sensation of death, the finishing of things, the sensation of creation—it's all there." He lay back puffing his pipe smugly. I wondered about him. Like a doctor, he had ceased to worry once the post-mortem had proved him right. The death of the patient was incidental. Four men had died in the creek only a short while ago. . . .

Jane had been subdued; the terrible event at the quay had affected her deeply. I think I felt the same, despite the drinks. The estuary had been a friend, a familiar part of colony life, always dependable, unchanging. Now suddenly it had become an object of menace swarming with predators, and our easy-going environment was turned upside down. As we walked down the hill to the bridge little knots of people were gathered, talking quietly; from time to time they would glance at the water. I spoke to Eric Phipps. It appeared that an ambulance had been sent for to take away the bodies and it had left ten minutes ago, empty. The falling tide had carried away the remains of the carnage. A token effort by Perce Walters to gather a crew to row out in a timber dinghy had fallen flat; nobody wanted to take the chance, and I can't say I blamed them. They could see no point in risking their lives to bring in a few bones. Had the plankton fishermen been Riverside residents it might have made a difference, but I doubt it. The colonists were scared. . . .

We took the track to Anchor Pool, Arthur striding along in heavy shoes as though out for a pleasant hike. He led the way and Jane and I followed in the wake of whiffs of pipe smoke. We reached the granite outcrop and scrambled down to the water's edge. The tide was low, the water murky. There were still a couple of hours of daylight left; the phosphorescence could not yet be seen and the pool at first glance appeared empty, dark, and dead. As we stood among the fallen boulders Jane took my hand and I squeezed hers reassuringly, although I daresay I felt as uneasy as she. . . .

Arthur tapped out his pipe on a rock and placed it in his jacket pocket, a curiously decisive action, as though he was preparing for serious business. He stood on a small rock and jumped, landing on a little island of boulders a yard or so from the shore. He crouched, peering into the depths of the pool. His thick brown hair had fallen forward over his eyes and he had an intent look, almost as though he was trying to will the dark water to yield up its secret. He stirred the surface with his fingers, tentatively. I saw his eyes widen with surprise.

Abruptly he stood. "Come and take a look at this," he said urgently.

I left Jane and leaped across the gap. He pointed. "Down there. Get low so that you can see deep. Tell me what you think."

At first I could see nothing. The pool was deep at that point and the slanting rays of the sun tended to make vision difficult. I shifted position so that I was looking through my own shadow. I caught a movement and tried to focus my eyes; I could not at first judge the depth of the object. Then I saw it clearly.

It was spherical, about the size of a football, and it glowed with phosphorescence in the black water. Arthur was stooping beside me.

"What do you make of it?" he whispered, as though the

strange sphere might overhear us.

"I don't know. I've never seen anything like this before. I'd need a closer look." I was shaking; at first glance I had taken the thing to be a face. . . .

Arthur reacted against my uncertainty. "Pass us a stick Jane," he said. "We'll stir this thing up a bit."

Jane looked around, found a piece of long drift-wood, and threw it across. She caught my eye; she looked concerned. Arthur had not our experience with the pool and we felt that more caution was required. . . .

He bent down and thrust the stick into the depths, frowning with concentration. I saw the stick, refracted, approach the glowing sphere. The point made a few tentative passes as he got the range, then slipped below the object and began to lift. . . .

Arthur jumped to his feet with a harsh cry. He dropped the stick. His hands were pressed to his temples. He was staggering, teetering on the edge of the deep water. I seized his shoulders, pulled him away, and we both sat down abruptly on the rough stones. He was shaking violently as though in the grip of some sort of fit, and I noticed that his right leg was pumping, the knee flexing rapidly and uncontrollably, scuffing a shower of pebbles into the water.

There was nothing much I could do. I sat and held him, waiting for the seizure to pass. At last he calmed down, opened his eyes and shook his head as though to clear it. His body still twitched to the involuntary jerking of his right knee: he stared at it in alarm, clutched it with his hands. Soon the leg was still. He exhaled noisily, shuddering. For want of something better to do I offered him a cigarette and he lit it gratefully, drawing the smoke deep into his lungs.

"Christ . . ." he muttered at last. "That was bad. That was really bad. I thought . . . For a moment I thought I was going insane . . ."

"What happened?" Jane's anxious voice came from the shore.

"I don't know . . . It seemed that I got some sort of violent . . . communication from the sphere. It went right through me, like an electric shock. It went for my mind and my right knee, like an exaggerated command to a nerve . . ." He broke off. His face was pale. "I wonder . . ." he said slowly.

Suddenly Jane screamed.

I was overwrought already; the shriek caused me to jump to my feet, my heart pounding. I followed her gaze.

The sphere had floated to the surface. It lay before us, bobbing gently with the ripples of the pool, rotating slowly with the current. I stared at it, transfixed. It held an aura of indescribable menace; it was obscene, fleshy and evil, and I had the impression it was watching me. . . .

"It's organic," whispered Arthur. He sat clutching a large boulder with both hands, as though reluctant to relinquish this grip on reality.

I forced myself to the margin of the pool; I lay on my stomach and leaned across the water. I heard an odd noise from Arthur behind me; it sounded as though he was whimpering softly, like an animal near death.

The sphere was a few inches from my face and I could smell a stale odour, like rotting fish. It moved slightly with the current and I jerked back, not before I had seen enough.

The entire surface of the sphere was in miniature writhing motion. It seemed to be composed of plankton, tightly clustered together. As I watched, the surface shifted constantly, glittering wetly in the failing rays of the sun. Plankton, gathered together in a tight ball. From all over the ocean they had come to this and other estuaries to congregate and die and, in dying, to be born again multiplied a millionfold, to go out to sea again and roam until, fifty-two years from now, the survivors would straggle back to the tidal waters and recommence the cycle. . . .

Even as I watched, a faint sheen on the water of the pool drifted from the sphere, spiralling with the current—new, young plankton about to commence their journey to the sea. The sphere was slowly sinking again. It disappeared into the depths of the pool, leaving a few tiny bubbles floating among the patina of birth.

I turned to Arthur. He was sitting on the rocks gazing at the point where the sphere had disappeared. His expression was unfathomable.

"You were right," I said. "This is the way they breed. No wonder I'd never seen it before. No wonder I hadn't been able to work out the life-cycle. I'd never have thought of this." In my sudden enthusiasm I began to think of the paper I would write...

"You've forgotten something," Arthur said. His eyes were

haggard. "This isn't just a ball of plankton, breeding. It's not only a womb.

"It's also . . . a Mind . . ."

SEVEN

"The plankton Mind evolved as a protective measure during the reproductive period," Arthur was saying, "in order to control the blackfish guards. I'm quite satisfied that it's also in some way responsible for the unexplained outbreaks of fighting in the colony and for the rioting fifty-two years ago. I don't quite know how just yet; but we've got to find out."

The Arcadian sun had dropped behind the hills; the deep creek was already in shadow, and only the pink-tipped trees on the hilltops reminded us that it was still an hour before sunset. Arthur had gradually recovered from his experience. Jane had suggested that we all go back to the Club for a restorative, but Arthur wanted to carry out a few tests first. I had warned him that the effect from the pool appeared to be heightened after dusk, but he shrugged this off grimly.

"Just an experiment or two," he had said, "while it's still light. We've got an hour. We can always clear out if we find things are getting too much for us."

So we sat on the rocks and Arthur, face set with concentration, thought about triangles and other geometric shapes while Jane and I watched him indulgently. Neither of us really agreed with his theory that the Mind in Anchor Pool was a fully telepathic being.

"You're going about it the wrong way," I said at last as he wiped his brow, which was damp with effort, preparatory to moving on to imaginary colours. "You're applying Earth standards again."

"Telepathy has never been encountered on Earth," he said.

"Perhaps not, but this thing in the pool will never have encountered geometric shapes, or arithmetical progressions, or colours. It's new, it's untaught, and it's blind. And the effects we already know about don't point to telepathy as we understand

53

the word. It does something else." I hesitated, then took the
plunge. "Let me have a try," I suggested. "A last try, then we go
home. I've got an idea. If I'm right, will you be satisfied for
today?"

He nodded and filled his pipe—in some relief, I thought.

"Now, Jane," I began, "I want you to think about something
—hard. Make it something unpleasant, which scares you. Look
at the pool, but think at *me*. Something which frightens you . . ."

I tried to open my mind, to imagine a blackboard on which
words were waiting to be written. I concentrated, but the words
remained unwritten. I stood and gazed into the pool. The light
was failing fast, and flecks like blue stars were beginning to
whirl. The Mind was groping in a nothingness at the bottom of
the water—a fresh intelligence with no point of reference except
the instinct of self-preservation for the brief month of its life—
groping to understand the world about it. I wondered if at any
time in the past such a Mind had achieved an understanding or
whether, with the departure of the plankton and the purpose,
it had died bewildered like all the others. . . . A child's mind, an
idiot's mind, which could hit out blindly when threatened . . . A
whirling nebula of blind awareness, spinning, spinning . . .

"Mark!"

A sudden image of myself falling, slowly falling forward into
the dark water—an image not on my imaginary blackboard but
within my mind itself, as though part of my skull had turned
into a three-dimensional viewing area . . .

Arthur's hand was gripping my elbow. "Steady," he said.
"You almost fell. Sit down. Try again."

I blinked and looked at him. I saw Jane watching me
anxiously. "It worked," I said slowly, hardly believing it. "I got
something. I saw myself falling into Anchor Pool, through the
thoughts of either you or Jane."

He regarded me closely. "Are you sure? Don't you think you
got dizzy for a moment, and saw a projection of your own fear
as you overbalanced?"

"No . . . I saw it from two yards away. From my left . . ."

"That must have been Jane." He sucked on his pipe excitedly.
"That's very interesting . . . Obviously you're on to something,
Mark. Care to give me a clue as to your reasoning?"

"It seems to me," I began slowly, "that the Mind cannot have an intelligence as we understand it—at least not yet, because it's had no chance to learn anything. It's a purely instinctive mental organism, with certain telepathic powers. These powers are random, not directed, and at the present state of development of the Mind can only be . . . second hand."

Arthur was interested. "You mean it acts like a sort of telepathic relay station? It picks up thoughts and transmits them without understanding what they mean?"

"I think so. And the thoughts relayed have to be violent and involuntary, because violence is what the Mind is equipped to deal with. Our strongest thoughts are those which occur on the spur of the moment, to the exclusion of all other mental activity. So I don't think that carefully prepared tests will work at present, although in a week's time it may be possible . . . We've no way of knowing how powerful this thing will get . . ." Again I had a frightening vision of Riverside in the grip of widespread rioting. . . .

"We must prepare people," said Arthur. "I'll have to get a message through to the Council . . . But what can they do? It's no use sending in troops to keep the peace. They'll be affected just like everyone else." He thought for a moment. "I wonder . . ." he murmured. "Do you mind if we try one more experiment?" The hills were black, the spiny trees stark against the skyline.

"We said we'd go," I reminded him. "Don't let's push it too far at present,"

"Not too far," he agreed. "But this may be the answer. The thing will relay powerful thought, we know that. But why assume that the thoughts have to be unpleasant?"

A half-remembered moment came back to me . . . Arthur was shrewd. He had insight into the human mind; he was trained that way. I thought I knew what the experiment was going to be. I didn't want any part of it . . . "Let's get back," I said.

"Wait. This is important. Believe me. Jane?"

She looked at him; her face was pale in the half-light. "Yes?" She was shuffling uneasily. She wanted to return to the safety of the colony.

"I want you to think hard. Concentrate. I'm going to repeat the names of objects to you, like in the old association thing. But I don't want you to answer. I just want you to visualize the

object instantly. Let the word form a picture. Don't try to fight
it. I want emotion as well as vision; so if I say 'spider', for
instance, think of it freely. A big hairy one. Let the horror come
through . . ."

Oh, God, I thought. Jane . . . "Let's get back to the colony,"
I said again. "We can do all this tomorrow."

"No. You ready, Jane? Right. Blackfish!"

It was there, a clear image . . . The men were thrashing in the
water; I could almost hear the screams. . . .

"Beer!"

Nothing. Or was there just the faintest. . . ? No. Arthur was
watching my expression closely. I shook my head. It seemed that
Arthur himself was not very receptive. I had a feeling I was
going to be glad about that. . . .

"Worral!"

Nothing. Nothing at all.

"Chorinda!"

I saw it, the yellow venomous snake of the midland plain,
twisting, sluggish.

Arthur said, quiety and decisively: "Love!"

Jane tried to check herself and gave a little whimper of
agonized despair as the half-formed, involuntary image slipped
out . . . I heard her sob; she turned away and began to scramble
up the loose rock desperately. She was running away from us,
away from the people and the Mind who were laying bare her
innermost and very private emotions . . . I tried to follow her,
calling her name. Arthur had hold of my arm; Jane ignored me,
climbing away frantically. . . .

"You bastard," I said coldly.

"Necessary," he replied. "And there's no need for her to feel
guilt about it; she's doing nothing wrong, is she? Did you catch
anything?"

I didn't reply. I didn't give him that satisfaction.

Jane was not present at the subsequent discussion in my
dwelling unit. I judged it would be some time before she had
sufficiently recovered from her embarrassment to speak to me
again. Arthur sat smoking smugly. He was pleased with himself;
his problem was by no means solved, but at least headway had
been made. We had a theory as to the possible cause of the
previous riots. Now it was a question of preventing their

recurrence.

"Can you imagine it?" he was saying. "The average human is pretty unguarded in the way he thinks. It's a form of release, almost—the idle daydream in which you smash the objectionable person on the jaw. And if we really analyse ourselves you'll find that we all have our dislikes, our acquaintances whom we would dearly love to knock unconscious, although we would never say so to their faces. . . .

"Even a mild character like John at the Social Club. Remember his scuffle with Will Jackson? They left the club at the same time; Will was the last customer and John, having suffered his conversation for some time, locked up and followed him out. Will probably lingered about the door still talking; he isn't the type to realize that not everyone enjoys hearing about his interminable sexual experiences. John was getting irritated. Some girl walked past, may be someone John himself fancied on the quiet—we're all human. Will began to drool and speculate obscenely. Perhaps John, at that moment, caught an image from his mind without realizing it . . . He emitted a sensation of violent dislike, which must have hit Will's mind like a sledgehammer. Will took a swing at him, infuriated. John's revulsion was amplified and relayed back to Will at full strength. Will continued to hit him and, when he fell, kicked him. Afterwards, Will wouldn't know exactly why he hit John; he wouldn't be quite sure whether John had said something to him or hit him first or what. It would never occur to him that he had read John's mind . . . And no doubt he was a bit muzzy with beer, too.

"This is the dangerous thing, this feedback effect. You hate a man; suddenly he senses it. Any dislike he may have for you comes back amplified. Your dislike for him increases accordingly. So does his. Once it starts, the effect could bounce to and fro, increasing in magnitude until a fight develops. Feedback. A Relay Effect."

"It's lucky that the deodorant salesman ran out when he did," I observed.

"You might have had a manslaughter case on your hands," replied Arthur. "From what you say, he was hardly a match for you. Fortunately, he was a complete coward. As soon as he experienced the violence of your emotions, he ran. Just as well for both of you.

"It's a pity there's so much violence and hate in our make-up," he continued thoughtfully. "This thing could be no problem at all, if only people could get along together. A sensation of brotherhood and love would be amplified—it works both ways. Any strong emotion would be relayed by the Mind . . ." He looked at me keenly and I felt naked. "She's a nice girl," he added, and I wondered how a psychiatrist could be so clumsy.

"All right," I said harshly. "It works both ways. Now let's drop that particular aspect shall we?"

"I just wanted to make sure," he said apologetically. "It's important, you know."

"I know."

"Right. Now, what are we going to do about it? Fortunately, the Relay Effect is not continuous, although my guess is that it will step up as the Mind develops over the next week or two. At present it seems that we can experiment in close proximity, while the effect over here at the colony is still confined to occasional breakthroughs, like a distant radio signal. So we've got to find an answer before things get worse."

"Why not just throw a grenade in the water?"

He looked at me as if I were insane. "And destroy a chance like this? A chance to study a completely fresh intelligence that has started from scratch? My God, Mark, I thought you called yourself a scientist!"

"I'm worried about the colony. I live here. I know these people."

"It would be better to evacuate the colony than to kill the Mind. Besides, you're overlooking an important point. You've assumed that this is the only Mind in the estuary, which I doubt. There must be many of them—and hundreds, thousands of others scattered all along the coast. You can't kill them all. No. We've got to find a different approach."

I felt ashamed of my suggestion. I felt a vague antipathy against Arthur Jenkins—maybe I hadn't been able to forgive him for exposing Jane's emotions . . . But there was something indefinable about him—I couldn't quite place it. He was right, though, to condemn my idea of killing the Mind. That would result—if carried to the necessary limit—in denuding the sea of plankton. Soon there would be no fatties left, and the entire industry of the coastal areas would be hit. To say nothing of the loss of a valuable food supply . . . Nevertheless, I felt uneasy about Arthur's attitude.

"The first thing is to warn the people," he was saying. "We'll have to call a meeting of the colony and explain the whole thing. Meanwhile, I'll send a full report to the Council so that they can take similar action along the coast. If people are on their guard —if they know they've got to keep their emotions in check or run the risk of a punch-up or worse—it'll go a long way towards minimizing the risks. A hundred and four years ago we didn't even have any coastal sub-colonies to speak of. Fifty-two years ago they were completely unprepared. Now, the least we can do is tell them what to expect. They'll be free to leave the coastal colonies for a few weeks, those who want to."

"At the same time we carry out a series of tests to try to find a more complete solution."

"That's right. We'll have to work together on this . . ." He rose and walked over to the window. I joined him and we looked across the colony. The lights in the windows shone with a friendly glow; it was difficult to imagine tht each unit contained people who, through no fault of their own except a common human frailty, could in the next few days become thugs, rioters and murderers. . . .

"Look!" Arthur pointed. Sailing into the night sky from the west, climbing over the dark brow of the opposite hill, came the first of Arcadia's moons, the huge Daleth.

We stood and watched; I was conscious of a grim foreboding. Beside me, Arthur stirred; he seemed about to say something, but remained silent.

Suddenly I knew. It hit me subtly, like a sly nudge, a quiet suggestion in my ear.

Arthur Jenkins was a latent homosexual. The bluff, pipe-smoking image was a pose. The man was queer. I detested queers. They were corrupt and perverted and they made my flesh creep. Just to have them around made me want to vomit. Importuners should be thrashed. I bunched my fists. By God, if Arthur—

"Steady." His low voice spoke beside me. "Take it easy, Mark. I said a moment ago, we're all human. We're all different. I can't help the way I am," he said quietly, "any more than you can. Don't blame me. Blame humanity, if you must. Blame the Mind that lays us bare. But we've got to work together on this thing. You see what I mean?"

"You're right," I said after a long pause. "Tomorrow, we've got to warn the colony . . ."

EIGHT

We decided to call the meeting for two o'clock in the afternoon; this, we thought, would give everybody the least opportunity for alarmed speculation. The notice of the meeting had to be put forcibly in order to ensure a good attendance, so we employed a loudspeaker van to tour the streets informing all that "a matter of grave importance to everyone" was to be discussed. While I was organizing this, Arthur spent several hours on the visiphone, bulldozing his way past every obstacle until at length he was able to speak directly to the Minister of the Council in charge of Internal Affairs. Thus was the Government made aware of the happenings at Riverside, and of the Mind. Arthur told me, with a rueful grin, that they had promised to look into the matter immediately. No doubt, he said they would set up a Committee which, after a suitable gestation period, would give birth to sub-committees. They might even send down a fact-finding commission. One thing we could be sure of: They would never move in time to build refugee camps inland. Riverside and all the other coastal colonies—some of them large—would have to sit it out.

Arthur also got through to his fellow teams in the coastal colonies and acquainted them with his findings; they promised to work along the lines he suggested and call back if they came up with any new ideas. Personally. I didn't at that time think there was a solution other than to depend on the common sense of the people—and I didn't place much reliance on that. We were in for two or three weeks of extreme nervous strain; a fair proportion of the population might not last the course. . . .

As we descended the hill and bore left towards the Recreation Dome I saw other groups moving in the same direction; it looked as though we were going to have a good attendance. I wondered how much they knew already, and how much they had guessed. I had heard some wild theories in the Club during the past few days. The common factor involved in all of them was the presence of Arthur and his team. They knew, now, that his work was connected with the tidal phenomenon, and they had guessed the link between that and the sporadic outbreaks of violence and ill-temper. With the illogical reasoning characteristic of any group ignorant of the true facts, I think they in some way blamed Arthur for things . . . And they knew the connection between Arthur and myself, so possibly they blamed me too. From that it was a short step for the private colonists to blame the Station as a whole—saying, perhaps, that one of our experiments had gone astray . . . The time was ripe to set the record straight.

I heard a shout and turned. The three lads, Minty, Spark and Yong, were trailing behind us. I was reminded of jackals and hastily suppressed the thought.

"Hey, you! No, you!" They were pointing at Arthur. They put on speed, shambling closer. Alarmed, I quickened my pace. Although there was no noticeable mental emanation from them, their manner was obscurely menacing.

We reached the dome and entered, moving through the crowd gathered around the doors.

There was a shout from behind—Yong's voice. "Go home, spy!" he cried, and I sensed hostility from the people around us. Arthur and I made for the platform at the far end of the dome. I wanted to get the meeting started as soon as possible before any more senseless catch-phrases were bandied about. I knew these people; most of them I liked, but I didn't kid myself that they would be different from any other mob if their communal anxiety and fear found a convenient scapegoat. . . .

The seats were soon filled and the back of the hall became crowded with late-comers. There was a buzz of conversation. I scanned the faces anxiously and was glad to see no outward signs of hostility—rather, a wary curiosity mingled with sullenness. This was to be expected. You don't call an emergency meeting for the purpose of telling people what they want to hear. These folk were expecting the worst. It was significant that the Research Station employees were sitting separately from the private colonists. . . .

There was a long table and six chairs on the platform.

Arthur and I sat down, joining Don McCabe and the other members of the team, Phil Horsley and Al Pendlebury. The chairman, as I might have expected, was the Reverend Emmanuel Lionel Blood, our elegantly-named rector who, I am afraid, is something of a broken reed. We had not requested a chairman for the meeting; I had merely informed Blood that we would be using the dome for the purpose. Obviously he felt he ought to be in charge of things. The clergy feel it is their privilege to be at the hub of local affairs. I noticed Arthur looking at him sourly as the Reverend tapped for order with a small gavel.

He then stood, and the meeting subsided into reluctant order. He introduced the team; for each name except my own he turned to the person concerned and checked his memory with a sibilant stage-whispered query. Despite the fact that he knew nothing of the details of the meeting, he then launched into a speech consisting largely of speculation. He was fully robed—he always is; the idea of the Reverend naked in the bath is unthinkable—and his scrawny neck rose from the black cloth carrying a wizened head, from which piercing eyes stared in predatory fashion at his audience. He resembled a terrestrial condor.

While he spoke of the need for us all to pull together—he assured us that with God's help we would win through this time of trial—I allowed my eyes to play over the audience. I saw Jane and Alan Phipps. They were murmuring together, and at one point Jane glanced up and saw me watching her; she looked away hastily. Janet Cox was there with her parents; she possessed an impressive black eye as a legacy of her incident with Paul Blake. This blemish on her baby face didn't worry her; she was sitting in the front row, and catching my eye, she winked grotesquely. I could see up her skirt to the crotch. I dragged my gaze away and noticed young Blake sitting in another part of the hall. A blonde girl, new to the area, was with him. Paul Blake casts a wide net.

Everyone seemed to be present. The three tearaways, Minty, Spark and Yong, stood at the back of the hall nudging one another and sniggering at the Reverend Blood's oration. I have always suspected them of responsibility for the incident on the occasion of the Bishop's visit. That day, as the devout crowd milled about the churchyard, it gradually became obvious to all that the board inside the gates had been tampered with. The previous day the board had read: "St. Joseph's Arcadian Church. Rector, E. L. Blood." Now, the Reverend's unfortunate initials had been repositioned at the rear of his surname. . . .

It was a childish prank, which had aroused the wrath of the colony. More recently I have begun to suspect the three youths of taking drugs, and other peculiar activities. Young Minty, in particular, is often missing from the colony for days at a time.

The Reverend had finished. He sat down. One or two people clapped vaguely.

Arthur was on his feet and there was a sudden hush. He coughed nervously; he was used to public speaking but this was a talk with a difference—the audience was involved personally.

He began by outlining the few facts that were known about the previous occasion of the phenomenon. He quoted a passage or two from notes of that period. Then he explained the purpose of his present research in the colony. One or two of the audience shuffled unhappily, and there was a moment's muttering. They had suspected it all along; they were being observed, like laboratory rats.

Arthur said so, bluntly. "The authorities knew this would not be a popular move," he said, "but it was necessary, they thought, and events have proved them right. We are moving into a time of great danger, and it is best that we be prepared. We must avoid at all costs the dreadful carnage of fifty-two years ago." He had chosen his words well. There was a convincing ring of menace about them, and the muttering died. Everyone waited to hear what was in store.

He told them. He described the first symptoms, his suspicions; he mentioned my work and linked it with the discovery of the life-cycle of the plankton. His voice grew in confidence, and he was dominating them as he ticked off the points on his fingers. Emotions could be transmitted to the object person via the Mind. The Mind was young and had not learned discretion in defending itself. There was evidence that the powers of the Mind were increasing with maturity. It was logical to suppose that within a week or two every person in the colony might find they were completely telepathic. There was no reason to assume that strong emotions alone would be transmitted by the mature Mind; it might be any thought. Every thought. He painted a vivid picture of their brains striving to cope with a bewildering influx of outside thoughts. He told them the worst, then he told them he didn't expect it to be that bad. . . .

He was finished. He sat down, and this time there was no clapping. The Reverend Blood flapped to his feet and asked if there were any questions. After a pause during which people looked at each other uncertainly, it appeared that there were questions. Plenty of them.

Eric Phipps stood. The Reverend called his name. He began to speak, his sheeplike face grim. "You've told us all this, Mr. Jenkins," he said, "and I daresay it's true, and we should thank you for warning us. But you haven't told us what the Research Centre proposes to do about it." There was a murmur of agreement.

I had expected this. Arthur—all of us on the platform—were in the hot seat. We had presented them with a problem. Now it was up to us to provide the solution.

"I'll take this one, Arthur," I said. They knew me; perhaps they would let me off lightly. "I'll be quite honest with you Eric," I began. "We don't know the answer. We could evacuate the colony, but we've got to face facts. All the coastal towns are in the same boat, and that means half the continent. Accommodation will be hard to find. Those of you who have friends or relatives inland, my advice is to get in touch with them and try to arrange for them to take you. But there'll be a terrific demand and you may be disappointed. So a lot of us are going to have to sit tight. Maybe the outlying farms can put some of you up for a while, but that's no guarantee of safety. We don't know just how far the effects will extend . . . One thing we do know is that the team here, and myself, and the Government too, are sparing no effort to find an immediate solution to the problem." I felt like a hypocrite.

"They can requisition tents!" someone shouted. "Set up camps!"

"I'm sure they're doing this right now. But you must realize the extent of the operation. We're not just talking about Riverside. These things take time. There's transport to arrange. Food and sanitation. It's no good leaving Riverside only to die of typhoid in the bush."

"Let's face it, Professor," said Eric quietly. "They're doing nothing. They're going to leave us here to go insane. They'll

debate the matter in Council, of course. I daresay they're printing
official letters of sympathy right now. Later, when all this is over,
they'll declare a day of public mourning. But they won't do
anything to help. Not one damned thing. I'd like to know something, Professor. Have the civil servants been pulled out of
Oldhaven and taken inland, or not?"

I didn't know the answer to that one, but I had my ideas.
Eric tends to be a troublemaker, but in all fairness, he was
concerned for himself and his family. His speech did a lot of
damage. Suddenly the audience looked ugly. One or two men
rose from their seats.

Don McCabe jumped to his feet and started shouting forcibly
in his thick accent. "Just listen to me, you stupid bastards. If
you really want to die, you can start a brawl right now. Because
it'll escalate into murder, believe me. You won't be able to
control yourselves. Didn't you hear what Dr. Jenkins told you
about the feedback effect? Now sit down, all of you, and be
quiet. Next question, please."

It was beautifully done. Don McCabe was in his chair again,
the meeting had come to order, and little Miss Cotter was on her
feet with a question. It was as though the Mind had transmitted
Don's innate force and dynamism to each individual person
there. He is a powerful man, with a tough, scarred face and a
shock of fiery hair. I've never seen a more unlikely psychiatrist.

Miss Cotter was speaking. Her voice was faint with nervous-
ness and I had to strain to catch the words. "This Effect," she
was saying. "Does it mean that all our thoughts, everything we
think, will be . . . available . . . to anyone who wants to listen
in?"

Beside her, Mrs. Earnshaw shot her a glance of deep suspicion
as she sat down. This was just one of the many problems that
would be faced by the colonists during the next few weeks. Mrs.
Earnshaw is probably the wealthiest person in the area—worth
more, I think, than even Ezra Blake. Miss Cotter is her paid
companion. Miss Cotter must be at least fifty-five—a washed-out
little woman whose sole object in life is to serve her employer to
the limits of her ability. No doubt she expected some sort of
recompense in Mrs. Earnshaw's will. Mrs. Earnshaw is irascible
and demanding, a leader in colony social life, a snob. Miss
Cotter has suffered this for over fifteen years. . . .

Arthur was answering the question. "I don't really think so. At the moment we are getting occasional instances of relayed thoughts. This may increase and, as I said, for a while we could experience general telepathy. But this would be so confusing that I don't think anyone need worry abut his or her innermost soul being laid bare. It would be more like trying to listen to five hundred radio stations at one and the same time. No, Miss Cotter." He smiled. "If you have some private Valentine, the chances are he will remain private. Just keep your mind serene, and don't indulge in any sudden, violent emotions."

There was a ripple of unkind laughter. I saw Mrs. Earnshaw relax. I wondered if perhaps Arthur was not as crude in his methods as I had thought. . . .

"And that's my advice to all of you for the time being," he continued. "Keep calm. Avoid powerful emotions. Avoid each other, if necessary. And one more thing. It might occur to one or two of you that the whole problem could be solved by bombing the Mind in Anchor Pool. This is not so; indeed, such a course of action could be extremely dangerous. For one thing, we don't know how many Minds are in the creek. It's unlikely that there's only one. And there will be thousands of others along the coast. The Minds are young. If interfered with, they hit back unthinkingly. We've already seen an example of this when some strangers attempted to net the plankton. I've experienced the Mind's retaliation myself, and it wasn't pleasant. Just remember that the Mind, if disturbed, can defend itself through your own brain . . . Thank you all very much." He sat down decisively and turned to Don McCabe, talking to him intently in that practised manner of public speakers which effectively precludes further questioning.

I stood up. The audience was struggling through the ranks of chairs and filing out through the doors. Arthur was now deep in conversation with his team and I felt a little out of things; I'd hardly had a chance to speak. The Reverend Blood was cawing some final words at the backs of his retreating flock, but I got the impression that most people wanted to get home and discuss things quietly among themselves. Arthur's revelations had hit them too unexpectedly for real opinions to have formed yet. Tomorrow might be different. . . .

I wanted to see Jane. I also wanted to have a word with Perce about the feeding of the fatties. My leg felt good enough for me to be able to resume my duties at the point. I left the team to their deliberations and pushed through the crowd to the door. I could see Perce outside talking to old Jed Spark.

"Watch it, Mister." Tom Minty was regarding me oafishly. "Hey, Professor," he said, a sudden leer on his face. "This mind-reading thing isn't too good for you, is it? I mean, it wouldn't do for your thoughts to be public property now, would it? Eh, boys?" He dug Jim Spark in the ribs and punched Billy Yong slyly. They chuckled significantly.

"What are you talking about?" I asked, annoyed.

"Well now, it's not for me to say, is it?"

"But since you ask—" Yong put in.

"As I was about to say, but since you ask, I might consider giving you a clue. About what people are saying. Other people, not us—we're your friends, aren't we, boys? But folks are saying nasty things about you, Professor . . ."

A little crowd had gathered around us, staying to watch the fun. I tried to shoulder my way through, but the doorway was jammed.

"They're saying it's funny how you've taken up with young Jane Warren, Professor. Mind you, we don't blame you for that. We wouldn't mind a bit there ourselves. . . ."

This was incredible. Here were those three young lads uttering obscenities in public, aimed at myself, in the presence of people I knew, and nobody was doing a thing to stop them. "I'm not listening to any more of this," I said, and again tried to push my way through to the door. "I'll have a word with your fathers.' Will Jackson was in the way, obstructing me. "Excuse me, Will," I said, trying to ease past him.

"I think you'd better wait and see what the lads have to say," he replied, not moving. He stood as though on guard.

"So you're not leaving us just yet, Professor," resumed Minty. I looked frantically around for Arthur and the team, but they had left by the back door. I was alone with an inexplicably hostile mob. I felt as though I was dreaming, a nightmare.

Minty's insinuating voice continued. "Yes . . . Folk are saying it's funny—disrespectful, like—you carrying on with young Jane and Sheila only six months dead. They don't like it much folk don't. They don't understand it. And so they begin to ask themselves questions. Do you know what they say? They say why should a man take up with a dead girl's sister so sudden? It's funny, that. It's almost as though he liked her best, all along. Did you like Jane best all along, Professor?"

"Don't be damned silly," I said. I looked at the stony faces around me. "Do you believe that, Will?" I appealed. He didn't answer.

"So it was convenient, like, when Sheila died, wasn't it? Accidental, of course. I mean, she could have been walking along the track all alone in the middle of the night and fallen in. Or she could have got her head hit, and fallen off your boat. Accidental, of course. But convenient, Professor."

God. So that was it. I looked around, and I knew. These people believed what Minty was saying. I felt a sudden impotent rage. I wanted to hit out, hit somebody—Minty, anybody. I wanted to prove my innocence by force.

"Hold it!" Perce was beside me. "You having a bit of trouble with these young toughs, Professor?" he asked anxiously. "I'm surprised at you, Will Jackson—and the rest of you. Why didn't you stop them? What's it all about, for Christ's sake?" He led me through the door. People parted reluctantly to let us past.

Outside, I told him what had happened. We walked slowly and I looked over my shoulder once. The mob was still clustered around the door, watching us.

"Don't you worry about it, Professor," Perce said. "Riverside folk took Sheila's death hard. They've known her since she was a baby. It was a crime against the colony, when she died. Nobody believed what the police said. Nobody believed it was an accident. After all . . ." He looked at me keenly. "Did you? So all these months they've been looking for the culprit, just waiting for him to give himself away. And you being her fiancé, and from the Research Station as well . . . And then young Jane hanging around you all the time—well, they thought it all added up.

"And Tom Minty's not a bad type, when you get to know him. He just hasn't learned to hold his tongue; he gets carried away in public, like Eric Phipps. If I had to choose between Tom Minty and, say, Paul Blake, I'd take Tom every time. He's a fisherman's son." He spoke as though this accident of birth constituted an impeccable character reference.

"But do you believe I killed Sheila, Perce?" I asked anxiously.

"No," he said. "I don't. But there's those that do. If I were you . . ." He hesitated.

"What?"

"If I were you, I'd keep out of sight for a while. I'd not show myself a lot. Just a precaution, you understand. It's best not to provoke people at a time like this, if all Arthur Jenkins says is true."

NINE

Perce was right, of course. I should have taken his advice and gone straight home, and maybe locked myself in, but I didn't really think it necessary at the time. There is an instinctive reaction after a man has been the target of mass antagonism. Immediately after the event he feels lonely and friendless. Subconsciously he feels that his recent adversaries represent a fair cross-section of the community as a whole. Nobody likes me, he imagines, immersed in self-pity. So he will seek the earliest opportunity to get among his fellows again, and having achieved this, he will be twice as pleasant a man as he was before.

So I said goodbye to Perce at the door of his unit, politely refused the offer of a drink, and made my way to the Social Club to ingratiate myself with people. I opened the door and entered, trying not to notice the sudden cessation of conversation. I ordered a beer, and John looked concerned as he served me; he glanced anxiously at the tables. There were about twenty people present; most of them had come directly from the meeting. There was no sign of Arthur and the rest of the team. Gradually the buzz of talk recommenced and I began to relax.

"Good for trade, these afternoon meetings, John?" I remarked. I had a craving for mundane conversation.

"Not so bad. Not so bad. You were at the meeting, I suppose? What did Arthur Jenkins say?"

I related the events, omitting, of course, my final unpleasant experience, and his worried expression deepened.

"I wonder if we ought to close the Club down for a couple of weeks," he murmured. "No sense in risking the place getting smashed up. People are in a funny mood. I feel as though I'm sitting on a barrel of gunpowder every time the place begins to fill up. And if Arthur Jenkins says we ought to disperse as far as possible, not gather together in crowds—well, it's asking for trouble to keep the Club open." He looked around the sullen groups at the tables, then his gaze travelled over the well-stocked shelves thoughtfully. He fingered a livid bruise high on his cheek.

The door opened and another bunch of customers trailed in. My heart sank as I saw several of the people who had prevented me from leaving the meeting. Minty was there with his henchmen.

"Well, look who's here," he said softly. I braced myself for trouble but he moved to the other end of the bar and ordered three soft drinks. He said something to Spark and Yong and there was a burst of coarse laughter. Will Jackson was obliged to stand next to me in order to get a drink. He met my glance with his arrogant stare, eyes shrewd and dark beneath the rim of the inevitable hat. "I'm surprised to see you here, Professor," he said loudly.

Fortunately, at that moment Don McCabe entered and saw me standing at the bar. "Hi there, Mark!" he called cheerfully, and joined me. Jackson moved away to make room. McCabe's presence was like a fresh breeze of normality in the club. His craggy open face was untroubled; his frank gaze wandered about the room staring down any furtive glances in our direction. I was damned pleased to see him, and said so.

"Yes, I hear you had a spot of bother after the meeting," he said quietly. "This sort of thing can happen in a small community. I should stick around the Station for a while, if I were you, until everything's blown over. I'm going to suggest that John close the Club, anyhow."

"It might be a good idea to impose some sort of curfew," I ventured. "And a restriction on gatherings. Like a state of emergency."

He dropped his voice still further. "We think the Government will declare a state of emergency tomorrow. Arthur's just been on to the Minister again, and it seems they're getting jumpy. There have been riots in Oldhaven and the other coastal colonies. Unless they take action quickly, this is going to blow up into something worse than last time. With immigrants and the high birth-rate, the population of the continent has more than doubled in the past fifty-two years."

"Do you think the Government will do anything constructive?"

"Only if we can suggest something. Otherwise, I hate to think what they might do. They might be panicked into almost any irresponsible measure. When you think what they *could* do, if they put their minds to it . . . I'm just waiting for them to think of poisoning the entire ocean around the continent. They could do it, you know."

"My God!" I was appalled. "They wouldn't do that!"

"That's what you think, but you've got a vested interest. You're a marine biologist. Now, think of their position. There's an election in three months' time. Our people are endangered by bug-eyed monsters in the ocean. Prompt, efficient action is required. Exterminate the brutes. Fill trucks with poison, drive down to the coast, pump it into the sea. Billions of gallons of nauseous stuff—it's unbelievable, some of the things they stockpile at the laboratories. But they always knew it would come in handy, and now they've been proved right. Acting with commendable speed and foresight the Government averts the crisis, and a grateful population re-elects them for another five-year term. Later, it's found that there aren't any fish left at all, but that's just too bad. Unforeseen side-effect. Never mind, they'll breed again, eventually."

The picture was all too convincing. I couldn't think of anything to say.

"You must realize, Mark, that the Government consists of ordinary people," Don continued. "They're not specialists like you or me. They're representatives of the average man, and they're almost as stupid. I mean, look around this room . . . No doubt there have been needless panics and blind idiocy in this very colony whenever a crisis has arisen. The Government is merely a Colony Committee on a large scale . . . Just look at them, now."

Obediently, I looked. I must say they looked pretty moronic, but then I was prejudiced by recent events. Will Jackson was ramrod straight in a chair staring challengingly into his empty mug, looking as though he was too proud to ask for another. Jed Spark had a full glass of whisky but was ignoring it, staring fixedly into space, his head shaking slightly as though he was in the throes of a cataleptic seizure. That took care of two members of the Colony Committee. Following old Spark's empty stare, I saw that he was in fact watching another member of the Committee, Tom Minty, who had been voted in last year on a wave of misguided sentiment which dictated that youth ought to have a say in the running of things. Tom was in the process of handing around sinister little folds of brown paper, which he and his friends emptied into their mineral waters. Grinning, the three drank, having cheated the old custom which dictates that if you want to be happy you must pay for your pleasure heavily in the price of beer. Jim Spark caught his grandfather's eye and winked. The old man sniffed in deep disapproval and took a draught of health-giving whisky. A couple of my own men from the Station were watching the scene; they laughed indulgently.

They disgusted me. I was feeling low, and the whole damned crowd made me want to puke. I began to wish I had gone straight home. Will Jackson was making rapidly for the bar. He had decided to have another beer. No, he wanted to speak to me.

He was shaking; his lips were twisted. "You bastard," he snarled.

"What?" Beside me, I felt Don McCabe tense.

"Just because I haven't been to college, you think you're above me. I tell you this. I'm a better man than you, Mark Swindon, and every man here will agree!"

Don had his hand on my shoulder. "The Effect!" he whispered. "Take it easy. They've picked up your emotions."

One or two people were climbing to their feet. Jed Spark stood, doddering with senile temper. Will Jackson raved on. "We don't want you here, you and your pals at the Station with your damned superior attitudes, corrupting the young girls in the colony. You think you're so clever that you can do anything you like and act as though you own the colony and everyone in it!"

I couldn't help it, the accusations were so unjust ... I couldn't help thinking that this was the man who ogled girls in the Club, who crept surreptitiously from window to lighted window hoping for a glimpse of a woman undressing ... This pathetic character had the nerve to call me corrupt. In my mind's eye I saw him as John had, as a predatory blackfish after succulent prey. ...

Tom Minty was beside us, leering delightedly. "You hypocritical old man, Will Jackson," he laughed. "Fancy accusing the Professor of being corrupt like you. There's plenty of other things we could accuse the Professor of, but at least I've never seen him taking women's underwear from clothes lines." He chuckled again and Jackson's fists bunched. Young Minty seemed quite unaware of the danger.

Don McCabe was whispering in my ear. "He's swung them around. The Effect's strong, right now. I caught your thoughts myself. Now let's get out of here, quick!"

I noticed the Effect too. The atmosphere was heavy with hate, at present undirected, but questing for a target . . . It was a time when one vindictive troublemaker could trigger murder. Don and I made for the door; looking back, I saw that the room had divided itself into two factions. The youths Minty, Spark and Yong stood with the bar at their backs, facing the uncertain outrage of most of the room. As I watched, faces gradually became puzzled. They were not quite sure what they were annoyed about, now that their antagonism towards me had been deflected, and even made fun of . . . The only target appeared to be the three boys, and they were treating the whole affair as a huge joke, ribbing Will Jackson about his alleged perversions. I sensed a relaxing of tension, just as I was becoming concerned about the position of Jackson himself.

"Wait here," Don said. He strode back into the room and had a quick word with John Talbot, who nodded. He passed among the Station employees rapidly, then rejoined me at the door. The whole thing was fizzling out; Will Jackson was blustering feebly but the aura of violence had died. "I've asked John to close up as soon as possible," Don told me. "I think they'll be all right now, but it's better to be on the safe side."

He was right, of course. I told him I would go home and stay there for a while. There seemed to be no point in incensing the colony by my presence.

Then he said: "That was a very strange thing that happened in there. Did you notice how young Minty saved you from the mob? It wasn't just because he picked up your mental carica-ture of Jackson. There must have been some other reason. I wonder exactly what he's planning for you, in the next few days . . . I should be very wary of him, Mark. He's a dangerous young thug, and those friends of his are no better. . . ."

People seemed to be going out of their way to offer me gratuitous and widely divergent advice concerning the Minty gang. I wondered if I would find out the truth one day. I had an idea they were merely anti-social, with a tendency to react against the conformity around them . . . But then, Don was a psychiatrist. He ought to know, or so I thought.

He left for a discussion with the other members of the team, and I walked slowly back to my unit.

The Arcadian Insurance Company runs a clever advertisement in the Premier City *Gazette*. Two years ago, tired of appealing to the common sense of the multitude (protect yourself, and the premiums are tax-deductible too!), they switched over to an emotional appeal. They showed a picture of a distraught family goggling at a burgled room. The characters were the same, the stock characters of any insurance ad—handsome, greying Dad; pretty Mum, surely too young to have borne those bonny children; Johnny, eleven (not yet transfigured by puberty into a herd rival to Dad); and Mary, eight, dressed like a Christmas-tree fairy.

But this time the family had slipped up. They were not their smiling and confident selves. Dad's brow was corrugated like roofing asbestos, and Mum's hands were hysterically aloft.

In short, they were not insured. Their reactions were spelled out in large type. They were shocked and deeply distressed to find their home ransacked, pillaged and despoiled; it had ruined their lives; things would never be the same; it was not really their home any more. . . .

But with a little forethought they could have had a cash settlement and everything would have been fine again. As it was, Mum would shortly put her head in the gas oven—just about the only portable object left—to judge by the expression on that perfect face . . . Which would be a waste of a fine, healthy woman.

I didn't feel like that. When I opened the front door and discovered the unit had been ransacked in my absence, I didn't think of insurance, or even suicide. Frankly, when I saw the drawers pulled open, the contents of the cupboards strewn on the floor, my reaction was one of fear. First, because it seemed one more instance proving my unpopularity in the colony. It appeared personal, aimed at myself alone. After all, it was my dwelling unit.

And second, because I felt the intruder might still be lurking on the premises. I had no gun. There might be more than one of them, waiting in the bedroom. I had undergone some harrowing experiences that day; my nerve was broken. I am a reasonably powerful man but, as I have said before, I am not a brave man. If it became a matter of facing the burglar man to man with the bare fist, I knew I would give a good account of myself; this was my home ground. In brutal nature, the advantage of playing at home is incalculable; I have seen a tiny wattlefish defeat a fatty four times its size for the sole reason that the fatty had strayed within the proximity of the wattlefish's nest. . . .

But burglars don't go unarmed. The man, or men, would have knives. Keen-bladed silver knives that would gleam in the sun's last rays . . . The men would stand apart, circling me as I waved a chair in futile defence. Then they would make a rush. I would get one as he came in. The other would get me in the side, first a prick, then a quick slide through the ribs, like an aspiration I once had for pleurisy. . . .

My knees were giving out. I moved weakly across the room, grabbed a bottle of scotch and slumped into a chair. I drank, I listened for signs of movement, sitting among the strewn confusion of my personal possessions. I lost track of time. When a voice spoke suddenly, I leaped half out of the chair.

I had left the door open; Arthur and Don stood there, staring at the wreckage in bewilderment. "What the hell have you been doing, Mark?" Arthur asked.

I was childishly glad to see them. I tried to hide my relief, but it must have shown. "It seems I had a visitor," I replied with studied casualness. I remembered the phrase from a thriller I had once read.

"I hope he didn't get the formula," Don said sarcastically. He had smelled the scotch and seen the empty bottle. He thought I was in the grip of delirium tremens.

"No. I'm serious." I stood up, swaying a little. "I've been burgled. I came home and found the place like this."

"Anything missing?" Arthur moved about the room aimlessly, picking things up.

"I don't know. I haven't checked. I never keep much cash on

the premises . . ." A thought crossed my mind. I walked unsteadily to the chest of drawers. I was light-headed; I remember having the inconsequential thought that the intruder was no expert because he had started from the top drawer down, thus having to shut each drawer before he could open the next—another tidbit of useless knowledge culled from mystery thrillers. Tag-ends of clothing hung from the jammed drawers like fish from a cat's mouth. I forced the bottom drawer further open and rummaged through the contents. I searched very thoroughly.

But the clothes I had taken from Sheila's bag were not there.

For a moment I stood stock-still, marshalling my thoughts. This, then, was not a random break-in; this was a burglary committed with a particular object in view. There was a pair of gold cuff-links in a box, untouched. So the intruder had come with the intention of recovering the clothes. He was therefore Sheila's secret lover. He would have searched for the bag in the dark and not been able to find it on the rocky banks of the estuary. At some time, attracted by the bright colour of the bag, the worral had taken it to its nest, where it would have remained but for the emergence of the Mind. The Mind had picked up my vivid recollection of Sheila and her bag, and my compulsive need for her, and relayed it to the worral, who had recognized the bright yellow image and been compelled by the strength of my own thoughts to bring it into the open. Practically everyone in the colony had seen me hand the bag to Officer Clarke. Clarke was talkative and had informed people of the contents of the bag. So the unknown man would deduce that I had the clothes. So he had come to get them.

And he knew that I would be able to describe the shirt and pants. Would he, in due course, come to get me?

Or would he follow my reasoning and know that pride would not allow me to admit the finding of the clothes?

My thoughts were whirling in an unpleasant vortex; I felt sick. I sat down abruptly.

"You've lost something," stated Arthur.

"No . . . It's nothing. Just a trinket. Sentimental value, really. It might be somewhere under all this rubbish."

"Look," said Arthur quietly. "You might find it a lot better if you told us everything. Are you in some kind of trouble, Mark? Is it something of Sheila's that's missing?"

"It's all right," I said. "Forget it." I looked up on hearing a heavy clumping on the stairs.

It was Don. "Nobody up there," he said. "No sign of a search, either. It looks as though they got what they wanted, and went."

"Mark knows what they were after," Arthur informed him, "but he's not saying anything."

Don regarded me searchingly. "Oh. Well, that's too bad. We might have been able to help. O.K. then, Mark, you play it your own way. We've got other things to attend to."

"The purpose of this visit, for instance." Arthur coughed awkwardly. "You're not going to like this, Mark. We're approaching the maximum tide-height now, and the Committee has recommended a few more evacuations. You're well above the expected waterline here, and you're a public-spirited sort of man." He smiled. "Your name came up as one who might billet a refugee or two."

"Hold it. Wait a moment." I was upset, I had a lot on my mind, and I was slightly drunk, but I still had my wits about me. "You know me, I like to live alone. I don't want a brood of snotty-nosed kids wrecking the joint."

"We're aware of that, so consideration was exercised in your case." They were both grinning broadly now. "As you know, billeting can be effected by outright requisition in an emergency, but it won't come to that. On your behalf we asked the indulgence of the Committee, bearing in mind that your work's important just now. You're practically a member of our team, after all. Which reminds me; we're taking a look at the Mind again tomorrow afternoon and we'd like you to come along. Don has a theory that we may be able to reason with the Mind as its intelligence develops. What do you think?"

"What do I think about what?"

"About putting Mrs. Earnshaw and Miss Cotter up for a couple of days. Nice quiet well-bred ladies."

"Not those two old hags. God!" My horror must have showed in my face. "I'd rather move out and sleep in the boat."

"That's an idea. I should bear it in mind . . . They'll be along in the morning. They'll be very grateful to you. Who knows, Mrs. Earnshaw might remember you in her will." Arthur hesitated. "Look, we ought to be getting along now. Would you like me to stay for a while and help you clear up?"

He meant the suggestion in all kindness, but I couldn't rid myself of the image I had caught from his mind the previous day. "I'll manage, thanks," I said.

"Suit yourself," he said stiffly.

They departed, and I began to pile the things back into the cupboards. I wanted to have the place looking reasonable for Mrs. Earnshaw.

TEN

I rose early the following morning and moved around slowly and carefully, struggling to retain a large dose of bicarbonate of soda and soluble aspirin. I pushed the vacuum cleaner over the floor and dusted the tables while Radio Arcadia informed me of the latest news. The announcer was not informative. It seemed there had been "minor disturbances" in coastal areas. Inland, there had been "peaceful demonstrations" outside the seat of Government by friends and relatives of the coastal colonists. As a precaution, the military had set up "information centres" at various points on the roads leading from the coast, and people were urged not to travel. The maximum height of the tide would be reached in six days' time. A well-known scientist from the Bacteriological Centre had held discussions with the Premier. A revolutionary new approach to the problem had been suggested; this was now being considered by the Government. The premier asserted his confidence in the people of Arcadia and considered it unnecessary to declare a state of emergency. He would be speaking to the people on 1400 metres at eight p.m. The news had been presented by the Arcadian Insurance Company, who wished to announce that their offices were closing for a period of two weeks in view of the annual audit. . . .

Depressed, I switched off. Immediately there was a tentative knock at the door.

Jane entered, carrying a bucket and an armful of assorted cleaning devices.

"Arthur Jenkins asked me to come along," she said, not meeting my eyes. She was wearing faded blue jeans and a thick roll-neck sweater, and she looked businesslike. "He thought you might need help in cleaning the place up for Mrs. Earnshaw. I hear you had a break-in yesterday." She dropped the implements to the floor with a clatter. "Do you need help or don't you?" she asked loudly.

"Thanks a lot, Jane," I replied. "I could do with a hand. I've made a start, but I'm no expert."

"So I notice. You go and tidy up the bedroom and I'll deal with this mess. Then I'll do some breakfast. I don't suppose you've eaten."

"No . . . Look, Jane. Do you think it's a good idea for you to be here?"

"What are you talking about? I've been here often enough before, haven't I?"

"Haven't you . . ." I hesitated, then plunged on. "Haven't you heard what they're saying around the colony? About me and . . . Sheila?"

"No." She looked puzzled.

"Oh . . . It's only talk, mind you. I don't suppose it really means anything. But . . . One or two of them are saying . . . they're saying I killed her, Jane." I couldn't look at her.

"What!"

"And that's not all. They're suggesting that I . . . got her out of the way so that I could . . . so that I could take up with you," I finished miserably.

Then I looked at her. Her face was fiery. She didn't answer for a long time. When at last she did, her voice was so low that I had to strain to catch what she said. "B-but that's ridiculous," she muttered. "How can they say a thing like that? You've never . . . you've never even . . ." She was crying.

I put my arms around her. She clung to me convulsively, held me a long time, then let go and stood back. She had stopped crying; her round chin had assumed a determined angle.

"Well, bugger them," she said. "Let them think what they damned well like. My conscience is clean." She flushed slightly as she said this, then went on hurriedly: "Nobody tells me what to do. And if you're scared of a few gossipers, Mark Swindon, that's your hard luck. I'll come and go as I like." She began to dust a shelf energetically.

"Just now is a dangerous time, Jane," I said weakly.

"Too bad. Now you go upstairs and get on with that bedroom. The old girls will be here in a minute."

"Hold it!" There was a shout from the doorway. Tom Minty was there, grinning at us, two suitcases in his hands. "I've brought the old dears' things. They'll be here in about an hour. Just performing my Committee duties, you understand. No wish to intrude." He chuckled significantly.

I wondered how long he'd been standing there.

By early afternoon we had got the two ladies settled in. It was decided that they should use my bedroom while I slept on the couch downstairs. It was no good kidding myself—I resented their presence. They were going to be a damned nuisance around the place. Mrs. Earnshaw was a demanding woman, not easily pleased; she regarded her billeting with me as an imposition—from her point of view. Every attempt on my part to be pleasant was greeted with a sniff reminiscent of the deodorant salesman. Miss Cotter twittered around unpacking, every so often bending solicitously over Mrs. Earnshaw, who sat firmly ensconced in my favourite wing chair.

I was glad when it was time to go to the Station to meet Arthur and the team for our visit to the Mind. Jane walked defiantly beside me. I was surprised that she didn't attempt to take my arm—she was in that sort of rebellious mood. Fortunately, there were few people about; they seemed to have taken advice and stayed indoors. We met Arthur and the others in the street and he asked me, rather maliciously I thought, how I was getting on with the old ladies. He then told me a rather disturbing thing. It appeared that Mrs. Earnshaw and Miss Cotter had tried to leave Riverside yesterday and go inland to a nearby town where Mrs. Earnshaw owned property. Ten miles out from the colony they had been turned back by the military. . . .

Eventually we reached the pool and sat down, the six of us, on the stones. The team had equipment with them in addition to their notebooks; there was a tape recorder and a portable steel box, which Pendlebury told us was a development of the encephalograph. He enjoyed explaining the machine. In some ways he is a difficult man to get along with for a person like myself who has lived all his life on Arcadia. He irritated me with his assumption that all colonists are bucolic farmers, centuries behind the times.

He looked at me sharply.

"Steady, men," warned Don McCabe. "There's a lot of emanations about."

My head had become fuzzy—a sensation of slight drunkenness, as rapid, half-caught images flashed across the recesses of my brain.

Pendlebury concentrated on his machine, twiddling knobs, trying to tune the thing in. The water of Anchor Pool was black, enigmatic.

Arthur glanced at Jane. "Care to try a few warming-up experiments?" he asked. "You and Mark seem to have some sort of empathy here. Just toss a few images back and forth to each other." After her last experience it wouldn't have surprised me if Jane had refused; but she nodded, frowned, and a picture of *Carousel* formed in my mind. Shadowy at first, it grew in strength until I could make out the details. A girl was sitting in the cockpit; she had long, blonde hair. . . .

I shivered suddenly. The boat disappeared. There was a babble of conversation from the others. They had all seen something; some had even recognized it as a boat. For others, it had merely been a white blur, but Arthur seemed pleased.

"We're getting somewhere," he said excitedly. "The Mind's increased in output. We don't need the force of an involuntary thought to get through, now. Did you see anything on the screen, Pendlebury?"

The dark man shook his head.

"I can't see what you're so pleased about," Jane remarked. "This build-up in power is just what we don't want. The danger from the Mind is increasing."

Arthur was suitably abashed. He had gotten carried away in the enthusiasm of research and was forgetting the main object. The operation was successful but the patient died . . . "Right," he said decisively. "Let's get down to business. Mark and Jane. Try to get through to the Mind direct. . . ."

The way he said it, it sounded as simple as switching on the radio. I concentrated, but I didn't know what I was concentrating on. I thought: Who are you? and tried to project this thought into the pool, but there was no response. I thought of a fatty, eating plankton. I visualized it approaching the Mind, imagined its hunger as it saw the succulent ball of meat. . . .

Jane gave a sudden gasp. "I can see a fish!" she cried.

"That's me," I told her. There was silence again as we concentrated.

Then, gradually, I began to get it. A formless whirl of dim, undirected intelligence, a sadness, a joy . . . An emotional morass with no purpose. . . .

"I'm getting through," I told them. "Do you remember, Jane? That time when we saw the worral? It's like that. It's the Mind's own thoughts."

"Yes," she said slowly. "I think I'm getting it too. Unhappy, dying, but at the same time full of hope."

So we continued, for a while immersing ourselves in the emotions of the Mind until at last I felt a sympathy with it. I felt that I was on the same wavelength. Then I tried again.

"Who are you?"

And faintly it came back. "Am? Am. . . ?" It was grappling with the concept of existence. "I am me." Not words, of course, just a mental admission of awareness.

"You are. You know. . . ?"

"I know. I am. I was. I will be. . . ?" The sadness, the hope.

"Blackish." I thought the image.

"Friends." A suggestion of encirclement, of protection. Comfort. Safety.

"Men." I imagined Arthur, Don, myself.

"?"

I tried Jane. I tried to picture Jane's mind. I imagined thought processes, awareness. It is extraordinarily difficult to project a mental image of abstract concepts.

"?"

After a while I gave up. I had a headache. "It's no good, Arthur," I said. "It just doesn't know us. It might possibly be aware that it relays thoughts other than its own, but it has no inkling of their meaning. How can it? We operate in an entirely different environment. The Mind just reacts. I don't suppose it's ever had occasion to think before. We're crediting it with too great a capacity, merely because of its telepathic powers. Those powers are simply for self-protection, instinctively to control the blackfish and any intruders. It's the old problem. We're applying the wrong standards."

Arthur looked stubborn. "Nevertheless, I believe that any being with intelligence is capable of being taught. It's just a question of finding the yardstick."

"But it can't even *see*," I insisted. "It's blind, Arthur. It has no senses with which to conceive space, dimensions or time. It only lives for a month, we suppose. It has no incentive to learn, no need to learn. What are you trying to prove, anyway?"

He gazed into the pool as though trying to penetrate the murky water. "We can't give up, not yet," he said. "This is our only chance. If it can't be taught, perhaps it can be trained. Somehow we've got to get through to it and train it to set up a block against the telepathic relays while still allowing it control over the blackfish. Then we've got to persuade it to pass the information on to the other Minds, all the way around the coast. Otherwise . . ."

His voice trailed off. I noticed a tic plucking at his cheek. He looked as though he were on the verge of a nervous breakdown.

Mentally I completed the sentence for him. Otherwise . . . we would experience rioting and bloodshed on a scale too frightening to imagine . . . I could visualize the other teams around the coast, working on the same lines and, like Arthur, coming up against the same insuperable problem. They were accustomed to dealing with powerful aliens on several planets. They had been instrumental in many cases in persuading such aliens to relax their powers and live in harmony with Man.

But supposing the alien is not aware of his powers? Supposing the standards are so divergent that he is not even aware of Man?

"I'm sure they're only doing their duty," I said hastily, as Mrs. Earnshaw's already brick-red countenance began to turn the colour of woad.

"In my day, young man, the soldier knew his place. He was polite, he was well aware of the fact that he was supported by the public, and he acted accordingly. He dressed well in a smart uniform, and you only saw him on ceremonial occasions. But these days irresponsibility is rife, and it's affected the army as well. We all know this; you've only got to look at the crime figures. So what does the Government do? It unleaches the troops like hounds to savage the public which supports them! And what you're laughing about, young lady, I don't know! You're typical of the younger generation. You have no respect!" Mrs. Earnshaw's voice rose to a roar of temper.

Jane muttered something about having a wash and bolted from the room.

I sympathized with her; she was young and the old woman appealed to her sense of the ridiculous. But I couldn't laugh. I was alarmed by the increasing danger of the Effect. This was yet another facet. Jane's mental amusement, which normally would have passed unnoticed, now constituted a highly inflammable fuel to the furnace of Mrs. Earnshaw's righteous indignation. This type of situation would be occurring all along the coast. Any slight divergence of views would be amplified out of all proportion to the importance of the issue. I wondered how many people there were in the colony whose views I disagreed with in some way or other, and I knew the figure must be near one hundred per cent . . . I thought of families in their homes and the bitter disputes that would arise—that were arising. Young versus old. Poor versus rich. Religion. Politics. Almost any topic I cared to think of. Even children's squabbles . . . Everyone's self-discipline strained to breaking point, self-control reduced to the level of that of an animal. . . .

Mrs. Earnshaw was watching me sombrely. She must have intercepted my every thought. "I'm sorry, Professor Swindon," she said with unaccustomed gentleness. "I'm a stupid, intract-able old woman, and you and your young lady will have to be patient with me. It's people like me who are going to find it most difficult during the next few weeks. When it's all over, I wonder how many of us will be left . . ."

I think that was the night when we all realized the extent of
the menace we were facing. The last rays of the sun angled into
the room, sparkling on the floating dust-motes, turning them to
gold. Jane came downstairs subdued; she had realized that the
Relay Effect was not so simple as it seemed. It was not merely a
question of suppressing any instincts of aggression. Almost every
emotional instinct had to be suppressed, because in nine cases
out of ten we react against people rather than towards them.

We sat in the room and drank scotch—even Miss Cotter
sipped a modest glass—while we talked quietly and endeavoured
to come to terms with each other and the primitive, sub-
conscious urges that make us all basically rivals. I don't think
we had ever considered the extent to which man is solitary. We
had lived close together in the various colonies of Arcadia; we
had been urged by the Government and our churches to work
together for the common good; and we all thought we had, in
the past, done our best for the community as a whole.

Now we had to dismiss all that as mere pretence and admit
openly that the human situation is competitive and that each
man will look first to his own interests. Once we had worked
this out, discussed and accepted it, we stood a chance of making
allowances for each other as we had never done before.

Mrs. Earnshaw was frank as ever. "I can tell you all," she
said at one point, "that in general I detest people. Sometimes, if
they are pleasant to me, I might for a fleeting moment almost
like them, until I remember that they must have had some
reason for being nice—because I am not a likeable person. I
know then that they are after my money, or my influence; whatever it is, they are expecting payment in cash or kind for the
effort of making themselves agreeable to a disgusting old woman
like me. There is no honest reason for anyone to be nice to
me. . . ."

Miss Cotter almost choked in her anxiety to jump to her own
defence. "That's not fair, Bernadine," she protested with
unaccustomed vehemence. "I've always looked after you as well
as I could. I've always acted in your interest . . . Don't you
remember, only five years ago I tried to persuade you not to go
riding any more, and you did, and you had that fall . . . And I
looked after you for the weeks you were in bed with the broken
leg. How can you possibly say I was acting in my own interest? I

could have gone and got a job elsewhere at any time during the last fifteen years. . . ." She was almost in tears.

Mrs. Earnshaw regarded her silently for a long time, and a flush rose steadily up Miss Cotter's neck until her entire face was scarlet. "I don't need to answer that, Elsie, any more than you need to blame yourself. We're all human, and the sooner we understand that, the better chance we'll have to overcome this Effect. Nobody can lie any more. Suddenly the human race must become honest, and about time too. It's easy for me, because I've always had the money to be able to afford to say what I think. It's going to be difficult for some of you. This young lady, for instance . . ."

Jane looked at her. I saw a stricken resignation on her face.

"There's no need to hide it any longer, my dear. Yours is one of the emotions we'll be needing. Nobody here is going to hurt you because of what you feel. You're young, and you think I'm an old bastard, to use your own language; but what you don't realize is that I *know* I'm an old bastard, so you can't hurt me. There is no harm in you, and there's a refreshing truth. So now there are four of us in this room, and before long we'll all know everything there is to be known about each other, and about ourselves. We have a lot to fear from one another, because we'll each see ourself through the eyes of the others, and we may hate them for what they show us. But you and Professor Swindon will never hate each other. . . ."

"These things can be one-sided," muttered Jane. I wished Mrs. Earnshaw would shut up. I wished it fervently.

"No, I'm not going to shut up, Professor Swindon. You're the biggest offender here, now. You know about me. You know about Elsie Cotter. Young Jane's emotions speak for themselves. But what about you, Professor Swindon? Mark Swindon, the marine biologist, the man who rationalizes on the basis of the cold fish he observes. Mark Swindon, who sees the animal jungle in his fish pens and reasons that human life is the same, and allows his fiancée's violent death to fortify that reasoning. Life is a battle, thinks Professor Swindon; and he is right—but he takes his reasoning too far, and forgets or ignores that we have qualities his fish don't possess—"

"Be quiet, damn you!" I found I was shouting.

"I'm a disgusting, opinionated old woman. I know. We all

know. But what do we know about Mark Swindon, the enigma? His thoughts are guarded. He deliberately thinks of inappropriate, meaningless objects, particularly when his eyes stray to this young lady here . . . Yet it comes through. I know what he won't admit to himself. I know that he is consumed with a strange guilt over the death of his fiancée. Not because he could have prevented it, or even because he was instrumental in it . . . But her memory screams in his brain whenever he looks at her sister. And that is why he will never admit that he is in love with that very sister—this young girl here, who causes his heart to quicken every time she comes near him." She looked at me very directly and I found it difficult to meet those hard old eyes. "Professor Swindon, it's not the image of Sheila you see when you look at Jane. It's Jane herself, this girl here. For God's sake, can't you realize that?"

Jane was staring at me incredulously. "She's talking nonsense, isn't she, Mark?" she asked unsteadily.

I could make no sense out of the whirl of emotions in my mind; I was unable to reply, to confirm or deny.

"Oh well, if you still want to try and kid us all, that's up to you," said Mrs. Earnshaw acidly. "I know what you're thinking, and I hope Jane does. I'm sure even Elsie here has some sort of inkling," she added unkindly. "You'd better see Jane home, Professor Swindon; Miss Cotter and I are tired and would like to go to bed."

I didn't really know what to say or think. I walked over to the window, drew the curtains back, and looked out over the lights of the colony. The night was cloudless; in the sky I could see all six of Arcadia's moons approaching one another from various directions, converging . . . The river looked vast, a great moonlit tract of black water extending from halfway up the opposite hillside to the flooded street thirty yards below. Over to the left, among the cluster of lights around the inland road, things were not going well. . . .

"There are two units on fire near Bridge Meadow," I remarked. "I wonder if I ought to go along and see if there's anything I can do. I suppose they'll have called the fire department."

"You stay right here, Professor Swindon," commanded Mrs. Earnshaw. "Those people will be the stupid ones—the deceitful ones who've picked hate from one another's minds and used it to nourish their own hate. The evil ones who've been found out and know it, and hit first . . . There will be a lot of homes burned down in the next week or two, but it'll be a weeding-out process; the survivors will be the good ones. I sometimes wish I were one of those. . . ."

"I want to stay here, Mark," said Jane abruptly, avoiding my eyes. "I think Mrs. Earnshaw's got the right idea. It's the way people combine in this situation that counts. We four may be a good combination. I think we'll accept one another's weaknesses."

So we sat down, had another drink, and started talking about going to bed. We were unable to dissuade Mrs. Earnshaw from a sudden decision to sleep downstairs, so we made up three temporary beds, locked the doors and windows, and I made my way upstairs.

From the bedroom window I watched the lights; the fires were still burning at Bridge Meadow, and I thought of fifty-two years ago, and the riots. Tonight was the start; somehow it seemed a milestone—but I was unable to visualize the end of the road. . . .

I thought of Arthur, and the sense of utter defeat I had caught from his mind when he knew that we had failed to communicate at Anchor Pool.

I thought of the Government, and I wondered exactly what they were discussing. I wondered whether they might pursue a dangerously short-term policy, as Don McCabe feared.

Yet I still felt there must be an answer. Tonight, the four of us had proved something. . . .

We had proved that if the Mind could not be influenced, then Man himself must adapt to meet the circumstances. Now there was a thought, and again I chased that elusive memory of the Social Club. I kept seeing old Jed Spark for some reason, his rheumy eyes staring. . . .

TWELVE

I woke during the night to a half-remembered sound of gunfire. I lay still for a while wondering if I had been dreaming—if, maybe, I had heard Mrs. Earnshaw slamming a door . . . Then I slept again.

We rose late the following morning. I was eventually aroused by a timid tap on the door. I mumbled a sleepy instruction to enter, and Miss Cotter appeared, slightly flushed, with a tray of coffee. She told me, with timorous defensiveness, that Mrs. Earnshaw had sent her up. She made it clear that she would never have intruded on her own initiative. I believed her; her eyes were darting about the room like a bird's; she looked everywhere but at me. I reckon it was the first time she had been in a man's bedroom. But the coffee was very welcome.

During breakfast Arthur arrived.

"There's a mob on the quay," he announced without preamble. "I think they're going to do something stupid. You ought to come and see them, Mark. Maybe you can talk some sense into them. I know I can't."

"Does Mark have to go?" Jane asked. "You said yourself that he would be better out of the way for a few days. What are they going to do, anyway?"

Arthur was pale. We offered him a cup of coffee and he gulped it down with the air of a man who would have preferred something stronger. When he replaced the cup on the saucer there was a nervous tattoo of rattling china. It seemed that, so far as Arthur was concerned, things were getting out of hand. He lit a pipe under the disapproving eye of Mrs. Earnshaw. His lips twitched agitated as he gave quick puffs of blue smoke.

"I really think it's best if you come, Mark," he said. "I wouldn't ask this if it wasn't important. I'm scared of what they might do. There was a lot of trouble around the colony last night

94

and they've started talking wildly."

"But what are they talking wildly about?" I asked, irritated. "I mean, they must have an object in view."

"I think they're going to dynamite the Mind."

"What! That's idiotic. Do they imagine there's only one Mind? Don't they know it might be in the power of the other Minds to retaliate?"

"I tried to tell them, but they'd all heard that ridiculous announcement the Government put out last night, and they wouldn't listen."

"What announcement?"

"Didn't you hear? They've finally decided to act. It's just as we feared—they're going to poison the coastal waters."

"Oh, God . . . So it's come to that." Suddenly I was unutterably depressed. Even the sight of Jane in her pyjamas watching me from the other side of the table failed to lift the heavy foreboding from my mind. This was the end of life in Riverside as we had known it. This was the end of the fishing industry for many years. This was the end of the Biological Research Station, certainly for my lifetime. This was the ultimate folly. "What's the mob, for, then?" I asked dully. "Why bother to use dynamite? By the time the currents have carried the poison around, there won't be a Mind left within miles of the coast—or any other living thing, for that matter."

"The private colonists aren't satisfied. Apparently the tankers won't be here for two days. They're working to produce this damned bacteriological jollop in their lab on the midland plain. Then they've got to truck it down. And it's got to be a simultaneous operation all around the coast, to make sure the Minds don't somehow warn each other and evacuate or carry out reprisals."

"Can't we hold out for two days?"

"The private colonists don't think so. Last night was bad. There were three units burned down and eleven people killed in unexplained outbreaks of violence. There was an attack on the Station, and guns were used. The Relay Effect was strong; everyone's edgy this morning. They say: Do it now, before anyone else gets killed. Why wait for the Government to move? Word's got around that they've blockaded the inland roads, and the colonists don't trust anyone any more. I can't say I blame them. I expect the same thing's happening all along the coast."

If you can keep your head while all around you are losing theirs, it's just possible you haven't grasped the situation, I remember reading years ago. The Government's road blockade was a perfect example of this. Intended to calm people down and prevent a panic flight inland, it was predictably having the opposite effect. The colony was convinced that the Council, secure in Premier City, did not really appreciate what was going on. . . .

"Are any of our people down there?" I asked.

"No." Arthur hesitated. "I hope you don't mind, Mark. In view of last night I took it on myself to issue a few orders. I've confined all Station employees to their units until this is over. The Station is closed."

"Since when have you been in charge of the Station?"

"Take it easy. You know the feeling between the private colonists and the Station. A thing like this could bring it to a head. We could have a war on our hands."

He was right, of course. I swallowed my pride with some difficulty. "O.K." I stood up. "I'll come down and see what I can do. But I don't think they're in any mood to listen to me. My stock with the private colonists is pretty low at present."

The tide was ebbing fast. The bridge was emerging from the racing water and the nearby trees dripped slime. A huge crowd was gathered on the damp stones of the quay; above their heads projected the elderly figure of Eric Phipps, haranguing them in his role of rabble-rouser. His voice carried clearly across to us as we approached.

". . . and I don't need to tell you what this means to the colony and the fishing industry that we depend on. It will be finished, friends. Finished. No fish will live in these waters for years. The trawlers will lie rotting in the mud. Our living will be gone. Riverside will be a ghost town."

I was surprised to hear that Phipps had realized the danger of the Government's policy. People had died last night, but this meeting was not, as Arthur had given me to understand, a panic measure. Phipps had foresight; he thought he could forestall the Government by his actions. I expect he had been in touch with the other sub-colonies along the coast. Groups like this would be meeting everywhere this morning.

His next words bore out my supposition. "They might block the roads, but they haven't jammed the radio waves. We are not alone, friends. All other coastal colonies are with us. This will be a simultaneous operation. We blast the Mind in an hour's time; my son is at present on his way from the quarry with the explosive. All along the coast, other colonies will be wiping out this menace. In an hour's time, our private thoughts will be our own property again!" There was a burst of enthusiastic clapping.

I pushed my way through the crowd, found that Phipps was standing on the roof of a car. I clambered up and joined him. He extended a hand to help me. His face was flushed with excitement. "Really got them going this morning, Professor," he said. "We'll show the Government how to handle this business."

"For God's sake, Eric," I remonstrated urgently. "Do you people realize what your're taking on? Let me have a word with them."

"Going to try and persuade them to go home and forget all about it? You're wasting your time, Professor." His manner had changed. He had sensed opposition. He became belligerent. "Friends!" he shouted. "Professor Swindon here thinks we're making a mistake. He wants us to go home and let the Government deal with it their way. We all know what that means, don't we?" The crowd roared. They knew what that meant.

"So here he is," yelled Phipps. "Professor Swindon, on behalf of the Government!"

The car rocked dangerously as the crowd surged against it; Phipps and I tottered unsteadily on the roof. I looked at the faces below me and saw only enmity. Phipps' introduction had ruined any chance I might have had of making them see sense. Now they were not prepared to listen. I tried. I held up my hand and began to shout as the noise died.

"There's more than one Mind in the estuary!" I bellowed. "There are hundreds of them around the coast! You don't know how far the Relay Effect extends. Kill a few, and the others will retaliate!"

"How do you know all that, Professor?" sneered Phipps. "How the hell does he know?" he yelled at the crowd. "We've found one Mind. That might be all! If there are others in the estuary, we'll bomb them too! How does anyone know there are more in the sea? Perhaps the Professor knows more than we do, but he's not telling." He dropped his voice significantly. "The Professor is known for having his secrets. . . ."

I saw Officer Clarke in the crowd. I jumped down from the roof in his direction. Hands pushed me, I received a blow in the back, I stumbled into his arms. "Get me out of here," I muttered. I could sense murder in the air; it lay heavy and vicious over the mob, a mental suggestion flitting from person to person, gathering strength, needing only one shouted word to trigger thought into action. The crowd was united in single-minded hatred of authority, and the hatred was building up minute by minute. Right now they had nothing to fear from the Effect. They thought as one. But I was the representative of authority, and I had everything to fear. . . .

For a moment I thought Officer Clarke had gotten caught up in the flow of emotion; in fact, he probably had, but common sense and training came to his aid, and mine. He began to force a path out of the mob. Reluctantly the embittered faces parted before us; the crowd was thinning, we passed though. Behind me, Phipps began to speak again. He was announcing the arrangements for the detonation. Arthur was waiting at the outskirts, looking scared.

My fear turned to quick rage. "What damned use could I be up there?" I asked him forcibly. "You saw what happened. I was lucky to come out of it alive! Eric's gone crazy. He's drunk with power!" It was the transformation I had seen before—once Phipps felt the crowd was on his side, there was no holding him.

"Sorry, Mark," Arthur muttered. "It had gone further than I thought. This thing's been planned. I don't think there's much we can do." He glanced around for our representative of the law, but Clarke was back among the audience, his face rapt. I saw the Reverend Blood being assisted to the car roof; he said a few indistinct words. As we moved away the babble of the mob steadied, organized itself into the droning notes of some hymn.

A hovertruck was coming fast down the far hillside. It slowed, navigated the muddy, narrow bridge carefully, spraying muck in the downdraught, then swept past us. Young Alan Phipps had brought the dynamite.

A number of things in the Arcadian sub-colony of Riverside were never the same after that day. Fifty-two years ago there had

been a disaster the extent of which was never fully compre-
hended—the records of those early, enthusiastic days were too
slight. Those were the days when the main colony at Premier City
considered itself young. New settlers were arriving with each
ship; many would take one look at the concrete and plastic
obscenities in which they were expected to live, spend a couple
of weeks at their Government-paid jobs, then strike off into the
bush with their belongings. All around the coast new sub-
colonies sprang up, new little communities where timber-built
units jostled standard plastic dwelling-domes at the water's edge.

The private colonist—the man who opted to go it alone—
came into being.

Before long, the Government in Premier City—an ugly town
to this day—decided that such decentralization was in the natural
order of things, and began to build roads. Disaster struck the
coast before the communication systems were fully complete; a
few faint cries for help reached the Council, but the nature of the
crisis was not understood and action was taken too late. This
time we were prepared; this time the planet had had fifty-two
years to prepare for *something*. Yet the very nature of the crisis
caught the Arcadian Council on the wrong foot again.

Next time, fifty-two years from now, it might be different.
The account of the Minds and the Relay Effect has been fully
documented, and I hope that adequate steps will be taken. But
the small tragedy which took place in Riverside that day of
retribution, after eleven colonists had died needlessly during the
night, will be remembered for a very long time. . . .

Arthur and I crossed the bridge again and took the track to
the point. As we walked through the first meadow we could see
the crowd across the river milling about on the quay. A dinghy
was being prepared for the short journey to Anchor Pool; I
could make out the figure of Alan Phipps passing the dynamite
down to his father, who was sitting in the boat while Officer
Clarke held the painter.

"Why the boat?" Arthur asked. "Why don't they just come
along the track and pitch the stuff in from the shore?" His voice
was curiously bitter. It was as though he had given up all hope.
I was shortly to find that, in fact, he had. The situation had
probed and found his weaknesses. . . .

"I think they've still got some sense," I replied. "They know the blackfish won't be able to rip the bottom out of that boat, so in that respect they should be safe. But they admit the possibility of there being more than one Mind. I think they intend to drift downstream keeping their eyes open, dropping a charge wherever they see concentrations of plankton. They'll probably work their way downstream beside this bank, then come back on the other side. That way they should be able to get most of the Minds in the river."

"They've got to get them all," said Arthur helplessly. "McCabe, Horsley and I examined this side of the estuary right down as far as the point. There are at least twenty places where there might be a Mind. They'll never get the lot. And after they get the first one, what do you think the other Minds will do? Somehow or other they'll stop the boat from continuing."

"You're assuming that the Minds are in communication with each other. We don't know that. It's possible that an individual Mind's only communication is with the blackfish, for the purpose of defence. I rather think they use the blackfishes' eyes and other senses as if they were their own. There would normally be no need for a Mind to speak to another Mind."

"I don't know," muttered Arthur. We were among the trees now: the branches were still, the whole valley seemed to be waiting. "I really don't know. Frankly, Mark, I'm beaten. I . . . I'd better tell you this, I suppose, but don't pass it on yet. The Government has recalled us. If we like, we can leave tomorrow, with a guaranteed passage through the roadblocks."

"Christ . . . I suppose this means that they're pinning all their hopes on the poison. It's a complete defeat, Arthur. This will set the development of Arcadia back fifty years . . . We've *got* to have fish in the sea; it's our prime source of food. And what happens fifty-two years from now? The same thing again?"

"I don't know. I'm sick of the whole stinking business. All I want to do is get back to Earth." He walked with his head down, chewing on the stem of his pipe.

We reached the granite outcrop and looked down on the rippling water of Anchor Pool. The tide was very low; mudflats showed everywhere, some of them exposed for the first time in half a century . . . I saw the skeleton of a large boat, almost fifty feet long, lying down the middle of the estuary like a fossilized dinosaur. Raising my eyes, I noticed a stream of people walking along the opposite bank, picking their way through the trees and undergrowth.

"Looks as though the whole colony is coming to watch the fun," I observed bitterly. They were gathering opposite us, too far away for me to make out individual faces. Their voices carried faintly across the water.

Then the boat came, drifting slowly downstream close to the near bank, Eric Phipps stroking the water with the oars sufficiently to give steerage. Two other men were in the dinghy—Officer Clarke and Farmer Blackstone, the thick-set man who scratched a mysterious living from the stony soil near the quarry. He would have supplied the dynamite; part of his income came from selling stone and chippings on the infrequent occasions when the inland road was resurfaced.

"What's your policeman doing there?" Arthur asked.

"He goes by the book," I explained. "It's illegal to dynamite the river, so he can't let anyone else do it except himself. That's the sort of reasoning I'd expect from him. Commendable, in a way. He's taken full responsibility."

Clarke was standing; the dinghy wobbled and I saw the fins of blackfish cutting the water all around.

"Careful . . ." breathed Arthur.

The boat was directly below us now, leaving the narrow channel between the mudflats, and entering the deep water of Anchor Pool. Clarke touched a match to the waterproof fuse on a stick of dynamite; I saw a bright spark, a thin wisp of smoke drifted. The crowd on the opposite bank became silent.

Arthur was staring at the scene. I heard him muttering, "This is it . . . This is it . . ." I wanted him to shut up.

Clarke was holding the stick at arm's length, the spark was eating down the fuse. Phipps took a stroke or two with the oars to swing the boat into position for a quick departure. They were directly above the position of the Mind.

"Now," I said, glancing at Arthur. There was a curious smile on his face, like that of an idiot child.

Clarke stood like a statue, arm outstretched, feet planted firmly in the dinghy. There was an inch of fuse left.

Scattered shouts came from the opposite bank. Phipps and Blackstone sat in the boat, watching intently, eyes fixed on the shortening fuse. Blackstone's lips were moving, he was saying something to Clarke. The dinghy had an air of unhurried expectancy.

"Drop it, drop it . . ." I found myself moaning. "For Gods' sake drop it, Clarke. Quickly . . . Quickly . . . Now . . ."

The shouting from the opposite bank had swollen to a frenzied roar of anguish.

Arthur was speaking. He was looking at me still with that crazy smile on his face; his teeth looked sharp, lupine. "Not now, Mark," he said softly. "Not now, not ever . . ."

Blackstone's lips had stopped moving; he and Phipps were regarding the charge raptly, with a queer serenity.

The spark disappeared. Clarke's arm was rigid, fist clenched.

The grass was cool against my cheek but a sharp stone had cut into my chin; my eyes were smarting, my fingernails clawing soil.

A brilliant white flash; a half-seen image of flung bodies twisting in impossible attitudes; a broken spine of boat lying in a momentary depression in the water; a rising, spreading shower of spray and jagged timber; then falling, splashing lightly—planks and baulks and things my mind refused to identify . . .

Then silence.

Little that Arthur or I said made sense, but one final remark of his stuck in my memory.

"We are identified," he said. "The Mind was able to construe the intention of the approaching boat. It was able to recognize the imminent danger from our own minds, and forestall it. It recognizes Man, now. And it knows Man is its enemy. . . ."

THIRTEEN

The death of Eric Phipps was a particular blow to Jane. A man not always liked in the colony, he nevertheless had his good points, and since Sheila's death Jane had spent many hours at his place talking away her initial sorrow and loneliness while the fisherman nodded sympathetically. Phipps and his wife had been good to Jane; I think they had always hoped that she would settle down with their son Alan. It must have been distressing for them when Jane began to spend more time with me on *Carousel* than with Eric, Alan and the trawler. This was, no doubt, the reason for Eric Phipps' growing antipathy against me; but he was not a bad man, and his dislike had been concealed until recently.

Jane also knew Farmer Blackstone, through Alan; I suspected that the man supplied young Phipps with explosives for his poaching expeditions in return for a few pounds of fish. I myself did not know the farmer well, although I had spoken to him a few times at the Club over a glass of beer. He was a rough diamond, but seemed honest enough by his own standards.

Everyone knew Officer Clarke, of course—a man of no great mental powers but considerable dignity and integrity, well respected by the colony. He would be hard to replace. He had been born in Riverside, and after having joined the police and left for training inland, he had returned to his home and remained in the colony ever since, a period of over twenty years, I believe. His replacement would be a stranger to us, and it would take the new man some time to get used to our rather lax, insular ways. His would not be an easy job. It had taken me several years to get used to the Riverside way of thinking, and I was still not fully accepted, as I had found out. . . .

The three women listened with dismay as I related the events of the morning. I had left Arthur at the Club. He seemed to be

in a state of shock, so I had bought him a scotch and asked John
to keep an eye on him—in the present mood of the colony it was
unwise for me to stay around. I had advised John to open his
doors for a couple of hours in order to satisfy the immediate
needs of the appalled colonists on their return from the estuary.
I didn't anticipate any danger from the Effect. I guessed that
everyone's emotions would be in sympathy for a while; the
shock would have united them.

I should have realized what would follow—how, united in
despair, they would admit themselves unable to strike back at
the prime cause of their sorrow, the Mind . . . But the urge to hit
back at something, somebody, would be overpowering. Soon, I
should have guessed, they would find a scapegoat. . . .

Miss Cotter was slumped in a chair dabbing ineffectively at her
eyes with a lace handkerchief. Mrs. Earnshaw ignored her,
grimly making coffee with the clumsiness of long inexperience.
Jane, predictably, was recovering with a large scotch. The whole
thing was second-hand and remote to her. It would take a day
of meeting people who were talking of nothing else, who would
describe in full ensanguined detail the dreadful suspense and
catastrophe of those last seconds in the dinghy—then the full
extent of the tragedy would get through to her. She felt a real
sorrow for the death of three friends already; later, the horror
would be imprinted on her mind by the eager gruesome words of
those who wished to share, and thereby dilute, their shock. . . .

Mrs. Earnshaw summed up the situation as she brought the
coffee in. "You can feel the misery in this room like a fog," she
said with forced briskness, pouring out. "The Effect has been
increasing ever since we got up this morning. I think it could be
dangerous; the whole colony is full of despair, getting worse all
the time. Feedback, you called it, Professor Swindon? It'll turn
to suicide before long. We'll have to talk the thing out. You
first. . . ."

I thought carefully. She was quite right, the emotional build-
up was getting out of hand. "I feel very sorry about the death of
Clarke," I began, waves of sorrow lapping at my mind. "But to
be frank, he once had me for a motoring offence which I thought
unjust, or perhaps overzealous." I forced my brain to think
logically through the fog. "Since then, I've never quite trusted
the man. If I discount the shock aspect, I think my sorrow at his

death is a purely selfish thing occasioned by the loss of a familiar figure around the colony. It felt right to see him around; it will feel strange to have a new man about the place, and this will worry me. I can't bring myself to feel sorry for his family, because I hardly knew them. And as for the moment of his death," I continued with sudden insight, "I think it was a question of mental substitution. I was scared stiff because I identified myself with him."

"And Farmer Blackstone?" Mrs. Earnshaw asked.

"I couldn't care less about him, if I must be truthful. A hard-working human animal. I don't thing I ever really thought of him as a person."

"Eric Phipps?"

"Recently I haven't got on with him so well, but I feel sorry for Jane."

"Your turn, Jane," said Mrs. Earnshaw.

Jane sipped her coffee thoughtfully. "There's no need for you to feel sorry for me over Eric Phipps, Mark," she said, "because my sympathies are with Alan. He'll feel the loss far more than me. It was his father, after all. My sorrow is a personal thing; I just don't want *not* to see Eric Phipps any more, like you with Officer Clarke. It's a selfish thing. So maybe it's not worth bothering about. But Alan's a different matter. He and his father were close."

Mrs. Earnshaw was smiling grimly, and I detected a distinct lessening of the aura of despair in the room. "What a lot of bastards we are. Don't you see, Jane? Alan's distress will be a selfish one, and therefore, if he were to analyse it, invalid. The only valid sorrow is unselfish, because that's the only sorrow we can't reason away. But if you follow the unselfish sorrows right down the line—from Professor Swindon to you, to Alan, then possibly to his mother—sooner or later you end up with some-one who's just plain sorry for himself. So there's no point in troubling with him. Let's forget it all. There's nothing gained by upsetting ourselves. People have died. So what? It's happened before."

It might have seemed callous, but she was right. This was the only way to look at things in the present situation. We simply could not afford to indulge ourselves with extravagant emotions.

Miss Cotter looked up. I don't think she'd been listening. She patted her moist cheeks with her handkerchief. "Oh, those poor men," she wailed.

"Shut up," said Mrs. Earnshaw roughly. "You're out of date, Elsie."

We sat for a while in the lightened atmosphere of the room, and soon even Miss Cotter's tears ceased. I couldn't blame her for her apparent stupidity. She was a sensitive woman and used to obeying instructions. In the emotional atmosphere her own feelings would be almost uncontrollable, because they would be reflections of our own. Now, the only sensation in the air was a dim residue of helpless rage which emanated from the colony around us.

"So, what we want now is a diversion," Mrs. Earnshaw opined.

She was prompted by a sudden, indistinct but definite notion of urgency, which I caught myself. I saw Jane look up expectantly. We heard hurrying footsteps outside, and the door swung open.

Tom Minty came in, his slow smile belying his thoughts, and his haste.

"Look," he began, "I don't want to worry you, Professor, but they're coming to get you." His eyes strayed to Jane and his grin broadened. "So it's true," he murmured. "She must have spent the night here. Why, you lecherous old Professor. Leading a nice girl astray like that."

"What do you mean," I asked sharply. "Who's coming to get me? What for?"

"Well, I reckon if you don't know, then nobody does. All I know is, they're on their way. Pretty near the whole colony, I'd say. Looks like a lynching party to me."

I caught a wave of distant emotions; my heart lurched. He was telling the truth. "But Why, Minty?" I asked again. "What have I done?"

He was still smiling. "Well, aside of despoiling Jane here, it seems they blame you for what happened at the creek this afternoon. They say you should have explained things better. They say you should have stopped them."

"But I tried! They wouldn't listen!"

"Maybe you didn't try hard enough. Maybe they think you're the expert on these Minds and should have pointed out the danger." His eyes took on a far-away look and the smile faded. "Or maybe they're just so blind miserable they want to kill someone."

"Professor Swindon!" Mrs. Earnshaw said suddenly. "Look at him! Feel his thoughts!"

They touched my mind, caressing gently, somehow serene.

Minty didn't give a damn.

As I had read in novels—the cold killer. The hired gunman who shoots and laughs and reads comic strips on the train home. Like the hackneyed simile, he'd kill a man as easily as he'd swat a fly. . . .

"No, Professor!" cried Mrs. Earnshaw. "You're wrong! It's not that!"

I could hear voices, many voices raised, approaching.

"The old girl's got sense," said Tom Minty, smiling again. "Like me. . . ."

"Mark!" Jane's voice was urgent. "You've got to get out of here, quickly!"

They were coming up the street and the swelling emanations were violent and merciless. I ran to the back door and opened it. I wondered if I ought to take Jane, then decided she would be better in the house. The mob had nothing against her. It was me they were after . . . I saw heads above the wall at the end of the garden.

"They've cut me off," I said, moving back into the room. "I can't get out that way." I looked around frantically.

Mrs. Earnshaw was ferreting in her bag. "Far side of the room, all of you," she commanded. "Against the wall by the window!"

The door flew open violently, crashed against the stopper and rebounded; there was a thump and a curse and suddenly the room was full of men. They saw me and their expressions hardly changed. Will Jackson and A'an Phipps were in the fore. Alan glanced at Jane once, then back to me. Paul Blake stared in at the window, an interested spectator.

"I think you'd better come with us," said Jackson coldly. He moved forward.

"No further," said Mrs. Earnshaw quietly, with infinite command. Jackson stopped dead, staring at the automatic in her hand. Behind him, the room was becoming more crowded as the mob forced their way in.

Jackson essayed a thin smile. "You wouldn't use that, Mrs. Earnshaw," he said.

"Wouldn't I?" Her eyes were cold. "Just look into my mind, Will Jackson, and see if I wouldn't."

Conflicting emotions flitted across Jackson's face; his expression became one of bewilderment. "I reckon you would," he said at last, slowly. "I reckon you'd kill an innocent man to protect a murderer. Don't do it, Mrs. Earnshaw. Put down that gun and let us take him away quietly." He glanced at the crowd surging around the doorway. "It's the whole colony, near enough, apart from his own men. And they won't be here. They're hiding in their units."

She held the gun tightly in both hands, levelled at his chest "It's the whole colony," she agreed, "near enough. But the colony is thinking with one stupid, frightened mind, mad with hate. To me, that doesn't constitute a majority. Now, before I put a bullet through you, Will Jackson, I'll ask you to call in those men who are waiting behind the unit."

The crowd had quieted. Baffled, they hesitated around the door, and I heard whispered information being passed to those outside.

Minty saw his friends among the mob; they lounged against the wall, eyeing the proceedings with delighted interest. "Hey, Jim!" he called. "Bill! Go and fetch those buggers in from the back. Make sure there's nobody left out there." Spark and Yong nodded, shouldered their way through the bystanders and out by the back door. Soon they returned with two sheepish-looking men whom I recognized as members of Eric Phipps' crew.

"Good," observed Mrs. Earnshaw. "Now we're all here." She craned her neck, saw the huge crowd in the street outside. "I'm going to keep the gun on you while Professor Swindon leaves us," she informed Jackson. "I'm not pretending that I can keep you here for long, but I'd like you to tell those outside that if anyone makes a move to prevent Professor Swindon from leaving, you'll get a bullet through the gut, as I believe the expression is. You'd better take your damned hat off . . . After Professor Swindon's gone, you can do what you like; but remember I'm armed. Jane stays here with Miss Cotter and myself. So my advice is that you all go home quietly."

Alan Phipps was standing near Jackson; his young face was drawn with grief and frustration. He looked from Jane to Mrs. Earnshaw and his expression worried me; I wouldn't have put it past him to jump the old lady in the misguided belief that he was saving Jane from some imagined fate. . . .

"Get going, Mark," said Mrs. Earnshaw. It was the first time she'd used my Christian name. "Good luck. I'll look after Jane. It's better that she shouldn't come with you."

"Right." I kissed Jane briefly, disregarding the angry murmurs from the mob. I paused awkwardly. It seemed that I was running out on them—but if I stayed, the house would be in a state of seige, and Jackson and his friends would make sure they had guns with them next time . . . It seemed this was the only way. "Ah . . . thanks very much, Mrs. Earnshaw," I said, and left by the unguarded back door.

I hurried across the rough pasture which passes for my garden, let myself out through the gate in the low wall, and trotted along the track behind the units. I saw a few faces in the windows as I passed; it appeared that not everyone was in the street outside my place. Soon I veered right, down the small alley between two units, and out into the street again. I went straight down the hill towards the creek. Glancing to my right, I saw the crowd milling about, some hundred yards away, but I don't think anyone saw me. They would guess which direction I had taken soon enough, and when Mrs. Earnshaw judged I had had sufficient start I expected them to be after me. . . .

Briefly I considered the idea of rounding up my own men from the Station, but reluctantly I decided against it. The last thing we wanted was civil war within the colony . . . I wondered what Arthur and the team were doing. In all probability they were up at the Station packing their bags in preparation for an early departure in the morning. I toyed with the notion of trying to contact them during the night, with a view to getting a ride inland in their car. I might be risking my neck for nothing, however. It was quite likely that Don McCabe, for one, would refuse to leave and would persuade the others to stay on in the hope that, even at this last moment, something could be done . . .

I thought of taking a hovercar myself, but my own station wagon was back at the unit and the garage doors opened onto the street—there would be no chance of getting away in that.

I reached the quay, breathless. The tide was completely out and the mudflats gleamed silver and black and viscous in the afternoon sun. Phipps' truck was there, by the cold storage some some fifty yards to my right. I wondered if he had left the key in the ignition. I paused for a moment to try and think things out. My next move could be vital. The sun was strong, beating on the wet stones of the quayside road with unnatural brightness; I felt as though I was an actor on a floodlit stage and moved into the shadow of the ships' chandler's doorway.

If I took a vehicle and drove inland they would know I had gone. In the aimless viciousness following my escape, fierce recriminations would be bandied about. Factions might arise, fighting among themselves or launching an offensive against the Research Station—a prime target. They would also feel bitterly against Mrs. Earnshaw, and the position of the three women alone in the dwelling unit would become perilous.

On the other hand, if I stayed in the vicinity, they would be united in their efforts to hunt me down. From my own point of view this would be uncomfortable, even dangerous, although I had confidence in my ability to avoid the mob. But from the point of view of Jane and the other two women in my unit, and the colony as a whole, it would be the best solution. The blood-lust would be directed, focused. If I could keep clear of them for a few days until the power of the Effect began to wane, until their minds cleared and they began to think logically again . . .

There was no other answer. I must become a hunted quarry, for the sake of Riverside.

FOURTEEN

Just occasionally it is possible to do the courageous thing when all instinct dictates against it. I left Phipps' truck where it was and made for the bridge on foot. I would not have been able to do this had it not been for the thought of Jane at my place. A few days ago I wouldn't have believed that Mrs. Earnshaw could enter into my consideration, but now I had developed a great respect for the old lady. I wished that I had known her better in the past. She, more so than myself, Arthur, Don, or any of the experts, had come nearest to devising a system whereby the Relay Effect could be defeated. Unfortunately, her method depended on common sense, and common sense is at a premium in a colony of assorted characters such as Riverside.

I couldn't imagine Will Jackson, for example, being capable of analysing his innermost motives and coming to terms with them, and with the motives of those around him. He would rather punch the opposition on the nose, and no amount of reason would dissuade him from indulging in that animal satisfaction.

Following the events of the day, it was more than ever obvious that the Minds were virtually invincible. To survive, the colony must adapt. But how do you persuade a man like Will Jackson to adapt? Or old Jed Spark, for instance? How do you take an assortment of humanity and turn it overnight into something unselfish and good?

I had reached the bridge and was picking my way carefully through the drifted slime left by the receding tide when I heard the chorus of shouts from the upper part of the colony. The hounds had been unleashed. I thought it likely that Mrs. Earnshaw still had her automatic levelled at Jackson, but that those outside, out of range in the street, had become impatient and decided that my death was more important than Jackson's

111

life. He was not a popular man . . . So they had broken away
and were bounding along the upper terrace, baying like beagles
in the unthinking united delight of the chase. I was providing a
wonderful therapy for the Relay Effect, but it didn't make me
feel any better. I was dismayed to find that my legs were shaking,
and I hurried forward, struggling to keep my balance on the
slippery surface. A sprained ankle would be fatal at this
moment.

About fifty yards away, uphill from the meadow, is a small
copse of tall trees and dense undergrowth. I ran for this, sliding
on the soggy grass. In a few seconds the mob would reach the
end of the street and would have a clear view down the hill and
across the bridge.

I reached the copse with a couple of seconds to spare and
dropped out of sight behind a thick fleshy bush, my heart
hammering. A worral regarded me curiously from a low bough;
it flicked its tail and scrambled up the trunk to a higher branch,
turned and stared back again, eyes bright and alert. Parting the
soft shoots of the bush, I watched the opposite hillside.

They roared into sight, a rabble of hate pouring out of the
side street and pausing, irresolute, milling at the corner. Then I
heard a faint shout and they swarmed down the hill towards the
bridge. I felt sick. I could sense the emanations from them—
murder, pure and simple, directed towards me like a laser. They
were unrecognizable as the people I had known a few weeks
ago; under the influence of the Mind they had blended and
merged into one violent being intent on slaughter. I tried to tell
myself that it was better this way, that, uncoordinated, they
would fall on each other like starving wolves; but I was scared
and already regretting my decision not to leave the area. I had
not bargained for the force of the emanations; they held me
immobile, concentrated hate like a snake's eyes. At that
moment I would have traded my soul for a grenade or two. . . .

As I lay behind my bush there was a crashing nearby and I
flinched, expecting a yell of discovery from some agriculturalist
who had been out tending his Arcattle. There were further
noises and a grunter trotted past, its young following in well-
organized single file. My hand closed over a rock and I lobbed
it at the beast, which fled with a snort of surprise. I didn't want
noisy company in the bushes at that moment. . . .

The mob paused again at the foot of the hill; some looked along the quay, some were turned my way. I saw white faces staring in my direction, arms pointing as though they had seen me already. Further up the hill a few more figures could be seen; presumably, Mrs. Earnshaw had released the hostages, who were now arriving to join the main pack. Suddenly I remembered my footprints in the slippery muck on the bridge. Soon they would find them. It was time to move out.

I eased myself backwards on elbows and knees, rolled over and twisted around, and began to crawl away through the copse, keeping the larger bushes between myself and the watchers on the quay. Some of the bushes shed sharp spines, which dug into my palms and tore through my trousers; I hoped they were not poisonous. A large proportion of the plant-life of Arcadia is still virtually uncatalogued.

At the far end of the copse is a narrow arm of the meadow. I sprinted across this and dropped among the rough scrub of the steepening hillside. I opened my mind to the thoughts of my pursuers; I sensed baffled hate. They hadn't seen me yet. I crawled about seventy yards uphill amid the knee-high scrub, then settled down again to observe.

They had found my footprints and were crossing the narrow bridge like an advancing army. Some of them carried sticks, but I saw no guns. In their haste to track me down they had overlooked the possibility that I might be armed. I wished that at least I had brought my shotgun. Their voices carried up to me clearly now.

"He turned right, just here," Will Jackson's voice. "I reckon he must have gone along the track to the point. He'll be making for his boat. We'll have to hurry!"

I had hoped this idea would occur to them. I watched as the whole mob broke into a trot, a seemingly endless column jogging along the narrow track, their faces intent as they passed below and within fifty yards of me.

As I lay there I felt a sly touch on my ankle, a caress on the bare flesh above the sock. I inched away and the touch became a grip, firm and insistent, sliding up my leg under my clothing, moist like the hand of a nervous nymphomaniac. I jerked my leg. The grip tightened.

A trickle of icy sweat was channelling down my spine, spilling over as I turned my head slowly, carefully, keeping out of sight of my pursuers below.

A sticker plant waved its tentacles immediately behind me. One spatulate arm—about six feet long and four inches wide— had a firm grip on my leg, while others gestured near. The whole plant was bending over towards me; I could see into the blind, gaping mouth, which undulated with the movement of the tentacles around it. I had the terrifying, insane impression that the giant land anemone was licking its lips in anticipation.

The crowd was still moving past. A tentacle caught my other leg, gently and persuasively, sliding possessively over the flesh and easing its way up over the knee, encircling my thigh in an obscene, probing embrace.

I was shuddering violently. I found I was moaning softly with horror and disgust, and surely they must have heard me. . . .

But the last straggler was disappearing into the trees. I rolled over, feverishly drawing my knife, hacking, slashing at the loathsome tendrils. Even after I had cut myself free the severed tentacles still heaved like snakes under my clothing. I tore off my trousers and ripped the disgusting things from my flesh; then I fell to the ground and vomited. And vomited . . .

Some time later I was able to pull myself together and take stock. I had no set plan. I guessed that it would take the mob over an hour to reach the point, find that I was not there, and return to the bridge to reconsider. I wondered if I had made a mistake—whether, after all, it would have been advisable to have taken *Carousel* and lain offshore for a while, occasionally venturing into the estuary to sustain their interest. But they would have given chase in the trawlers. I couldn't have outrun them, with my little $5\frac{1}{2}$ horse-power against their throbbing diesels. At the time it didn't occur to me that I could have taken a trawler myself.

For a while I watched the glittering domes of the colony, considering my next move.

At first the streets remained empty, and the colony had an abandoned appearance in the afternoon sun. After a few minutes people began to move about. There was something slow and tired-looking about them, as though they were in a state of shock. These would be the ones who had resisted the mass impulse to join the chase, and I wondered what unknown block they had been able to set up in their minds. Maybe they reasoned along the lines of Mrs. Earnshaw, or maybe they had succeeded in hypnotizing themselves into a state of euphoria through which the emanations could not penetrate. I wished I knew. Any one of those people could hold the answer to the peril facing Arcadia. . . .

Soon three figures came around the top corner of the hill; by their shambling gait and the burst of irresponsible laughter that reached me, I took them to be Minty and his gang. I was unable to understand Minty's viewpoint. At times he had seemed definitely antagonistic towards me, but when the heat had been on he had taken my side to a degree. It seemed that somehow, despite my original impressions of him, he and his friends were almost in the nature of non-violent onlookers—neutrals. They observed, they got a vicarious enjoyment from the stupidity going on around them, but they refused to participate.

I didn't trust them. They were loping down the hill now, and there was a purpose about them. They were coming to find me, and they would not go rushing blindly down the track to the point like their predecessors.

I began to crawl uphill again and soon reached the brow of the ridge that runs parallel to the estuary, all the way to the point. Cover consisted of rough scrub on grass close-cropped by Arcattle, and it was sparse. The ridge was swept by the prevailing winds; the few trees were stunted and forced into flying, curved aerodynamic outlines.

I descended the far side of the ridge and, out of sight of the colony, began to run steadily across the slope in the direction of the sea. To my left the ground fell away before flattening out to the wide inland valley dotted with the dome complexes of agricultural sub-stations and private farms. The road twisted among the fields, following the approximate course of one of the tributaries of the river. A spur of the road ran below and terminated at the foot of the ridge half a mile ahead. There was a huddle of derelict buildings, the late Farmer Blackstone's place, and the gaunt scar of the granite quarry.

I hurried on; the sun was slipping low and my side of the ridge was in shadow. Soon I was scrambling around the precipitous edge of the quarry, skirting the rusted wire fence erected by the

farmer in an abortive attempt to prevent his Arcattle from
grazing in suicidal fashion on the lip of the thirty-foot drop.
Then I was in open ground, in view of the sea. Later I began to
climb again, and before long I was crawling, easing my head
cautiously over the crest of the rise.

The crowd was milling undecidedly at the edge of the cliff,
watching the rowboat pull from the shore. Four men were in it.
Beyond them, the sea was gunmetal in the low rays of the sun,
and the dark shapes of the boats projected harshly from the
smooth surface, alone and desolate, like wrecks. Before long the
men were boarding my boat. I felt a flush of inappropriate
annoyance.

Then they climbed back into the dinghy and began to row for
the shore. Those at the cliff-top were shouting angrily; they
wanted the men to board each trawler and search it thoroughly.
Faint replies came from the rowboat. I could guess what had
happened. In their haste and anger at not finding me at the point
they had rowed off in the dinghy without further considering the
matter. On boarding *Carousel* they realized I would not be
there, because there had never been more than one rowboat at
the point. If I had boarded any of the ships, I would already have
taken it. These men were used to the sea and they knew me; they
would guess that I would never have attempted to swim to the
boats, with the water teeming with blackfish and a dinghy at
hand. They were wasting their time. The crowd at the cliff-top
had not understood this and were infuriated at the others for
apparently giving up.

The boat was beached, the men were swung to the top of the
cliff, and a furious altercation took place. Women on the
outskirts of the crowd were waving their fists and berating the
men shrilly; the men around the small crane had advanced
threateningly on the returned boarding party. Things were
getting ugly.

There was a soft footstep beside me and my throat constricted.

"Getting a grandstand view, Professor?" The cold amused
voice of Minty sounded like a knell.

The three of them stood there: Minty, Yong and Spark. They
looked at me. Then their eyes moved to the scene at the cliff-top
a hundred yards away.

"It looks almost as if it might get out of hand soon," observed

Minty. "Now let's think this thing out carefully, boys, shall we? All those people really want is the Professor here. And they'd better have him quick, otherwise somebody's going to get hurt. Right?"

Wolfish grins of agreement from the other two.

"Oh dear. Look at that," said Minty mildly.

A fight had broken out. The din of the mob had increased and the emanations were turbulent. The youths stood above me, apparently unaffected, watching, interested.

A wailing scream of despair as a figure, flailing air, teetered on the brink of the drop for an age before he fell backwards, dropping out of sight. I felt ill. That death was on my account.

"Right, lads," said Minty. "Let's go and break it up before anyone else gets damaged. Pity, but there it is. Must preserve human life."

Yelling, the three youths bounded down the hillside while I watched with the sickness of despair. The attention of the crowd was distracted momentarily. Heads turned, the protagonists paused in their scuffle. Minty and his friends forced their way into the centre; I heard his voice addressing them urgently, but I couldn't catch the words. All I could do was wait. I couldn't hope to outrun them all.

Minty was pointing back along the track. A few men began to run; the others paused to hear the youth's final words, then followed. Soon a stream of humanity was hurrying back along the track to the colony.

Minty had diverted them, sent them all in the wrong direction. Why? Puzzled but unutterably relieved, I rose to my feet and headed for the quarry.

The sloping hillside ran down to the foot of the quarry, which was a wedge-shaped bite sixty feet long and wide and thirty feet high. Stickers clutched at my legs as I descended, and I shuddered involuntarily. The floor of the quarry was littered with assorted items of rusting equipment—long-forgotten legacies of the days when the road inland was first built and the demand for hardcore had made Farmer Blackstone's predecessor a comparatively well-off man. Since those days the farm buildings had deteriorated steadily. Shingle-covered and ramshackle, they backed onto one side of the quarry. Here and there the blackened shingles had peeled away from the walls, and the gaps had been repaired with nailed sheets of tarpaulin and incongruously white ply squares. Similar patchwork decorated the single small storage dome.

I was banking on the place being deserted. In the new mood of honesty engendered by Mrs. Earnshaw, I felt no compunction in using it as a temporary hideout. The hillside was deep in twilight, and the small triangular webs of the kite-bugs veered and soared among the trees as they blindly trawled the evening air like phosphorescent bats for small prey. The cluster of shacks and outhouses looked menacing and mysterious, but that was all to the good. A number of the colonists are incredibly superstitious, and I deemed it unlikely that, following the death of the farmer, anyone would come prowling around in the night.

I pushed open the door to the main farmhouse and entered. I struck a match and looked around. There was a smell of stale food. The large combined kitchen and living room looked much as I had expected from a man unable or unwilling to buy a permaplast dwelling dome—a clutter of ancient furniture, walls grey with mildewed whitewash and decorated with a few faded prints, a worn brown carpet covering most of the floor. There was a lamp on the table among the remains of the farmer's last breakfast; I lit it and climbed the stairs to the bedroom. This was sparsely furnished but tidy, and I closed the curtains before investigating further. There was always the possibility that someone might see the light from the road and report it back to the colony.

The bed had been made before its deceased occupant had left for the day. After searching the drawers and cupboards in the vain hope of finding a gun, I lay down and was asleep within seconds.

I was wakened next morning by the bellowing of livestock outside the window. This was something I had not allowed for. No doubt the animals followed some set routine as to feeding and milking, but I was ignorant as to how to set about these tasks. It occurred to me as I lay on the bed, with the new sun illuminating the room, that someone else might have thought of this. It was quite possible that some kindly person in the colony —there must be some left—would think to get up early and come across, with a view to looking after the animals until the sale of effects took place. In which case they would be here soon.

I had a quick, final look around the bedroom without success and went downstairs. A further search revealed no firearms of any sort—the farmer appeared to have been a pacifist. I did find some food, however, and cooked up a heavy meal of bacon, eggs sausages, and anything else I could lay my hands on to sustain myself during what promised to be a hard day in the open. The bacon, home-cured, had a slightly bitter tang, and I hesitated before eating it. It was grunter meat, rather than adapted terrestrial pig; while it is perfectly safe, eating this Arcadian meat is viewed with prejudice.

I could see no point in washing up, so I dropped a few further items of food in a bag and left. The back door of the house gave onto a small yard bounded by sheds; a door was ajar, and I saw that one small building appeared to be a workshop of sorts. I went inside and searched the drawers beneath the workbench. The variety of contents was remarkable, but there was little of any practical use to a man on the run. I did find a short dagger-like knife, however, which I stuck in my belt. I opened the door of the only dome and was confronted by a pile of bulging sacks.

Sitting on the pile, holding a shotgun levelled at my stomach, was Tom Minty.

"Well, Professor," he said easily. "Fancy seeing you here. Sit down if you will, I want to have a word with you."

FIFTEEN

I stared at him for some seconds, wondering how the hell he had found me, wondering what his intentions were. There was something businesslike about the way he held the shotgun. Following my gaze, Minty regarded the gun with exaggerated interest, as though he were seeing it for the first time.

"Impressive device, Professor," he observed. "Murderous, really. Do a lot of damage with a gadget like this. Put a hole clean through a man's stomach, if it went off. Don't worry, I've handled it before. Still, no sense in taking chances is there?"

To my surprise and relief he laid the shotgun beside him and grinned up at me pleasantly. "Sit down," he said again. I sat down abruptly on a bulging sack.

"Sorry to worry you like that," he continued. "But there are those who'd say that what I'm doing here isn't legal, I knew you were here, but I had to be sure, see?"

"I'm afraid I don't see."

He laughed. "Just a word of advice, Professor. Just because you don't see anyone around the place, don't get the idea you're safe and hidden. I just came up from the colony by the shortcut over the ridge. I could tell you were here from a mile range—your thoughts were yelling in my mind like a hunted worral. They might even be able to hear you in the colony, for all I know. You've got problems, Professor. You're frightened all the time."

"I can't help that."

His face grew cunning. "Ah, but you could. Never mind, we'll talk about that later. I'll leave the gun with you, just in case."

"What the hell's going on, Minty?" I asked. "What's your game? Are you on my side or not?" I couldn't make him out at all.

"Call me neutral. I'm not really interested in seeing people get

120

hurt; it's sort of against my philosophy. Neutral, that's me. Reach into my mind, Professor, and tell me what you see."

I stared at him and concentrated, knowing that the very fact of my having to concentrate was odd. All morning I had been receiving indistinct emanations from the colony, yet Minty's sudden appearance had taken me completely by surprise. Then I caught his emissions—faint, calm, untroubled. "Don't worry, Professor," he said softly. "Take it easy, like me. Your mind's like a fatty with blackfish all around. But hadn't you noticed, you don't make me scared?"

I blinked, puzzled, and I'd lost him again.

"Mrs. Earnshaw's got the right idea," he said. "I had a long talk with her. She's quite a woman, for an old one. She told me about the way you and Jane and her kept away the uglies by facing facts, by just being honest with each other. Pity it doesn't work for everyone . . . Tell me this, Professor." He leaned forward, staring at me hard. "Did you kill Sheila?"

The question filled my mind with unreasoning guilt. Maybe it was the unexpectedness of it, maybe it was the fact that I knew the colony thought me a murderer. It was a moment of sheer uncontrolled horror and helplessness and rage at my own stupid reactions—and I wondered if I had a chance of getting the gun before Minty.

But he leaned back. "O.K., I'm satisfied," he said. "So they're all wrong. But why do you want to prove they're right?" he asked. "There's something funny in your mind, something I can't reach. Almost as if you're glad she's dead, as though you hate her now. What happened, Professor? You didn't kill her, I can tell that. Why do you feel so guilty about it? What went wrong?"

There seemed to be nothing I could hide from this youth, and I knew that in a moment I would be projecting an involuntary image of Sheila and some man running about the hillside, laughing . . . And with the fear, the thought was half-way out, and Minty's eyes widened.

"How's Jane?" I asked abruptly. "Have you seen her?"

He hesitated, still trying to catch the broken image. "Yes," he said finally. "She's O.K. She and the two old ladies are all alone in your place, and nobody's bothering them. It's still you they're after, and if it wasn't for the news this morning, they'd be here already."

"News? The radio?"

"Oh, yes. Seems as if things are moving. Just as well too, because there was a lot of trouble last night after the mob got back to the colony and couldn't find you. They blamed Perce Walters for some reason, maybe because they could tell he was in sympathy with you, so to speak. So a group of them went up to his house to smoke him out."

"Set fire to his place, you mean?" I was horrified; I had forgotten Perce's previous support for me. Naturally they would pick up his emanations . . . Like the houses of many of the private colonists, Perce's place was constructed of Arcadian timber.

Minty chuckled. "They tried, but they weren't strong enough. Perce is well-liked. He didn't even have to shoot. He came out of that house like a grunter charging and smashed the first man's head open with the butt of his gun. The others took fright; besides, Perce's supporters arrived. So there was a bit of a battle and the air was thick with this awful feeling of hate—enough to burn your brains out. But nobody had any weapons, and Perce disappeared—sensibly, and everybody got beaten up and so tired they forgot in the end what it was all about and went home, those that could walk. It was interesting while it lasted, but kind of inconclusive. They might have another go today but I doubt it, in view of the news."

"What news?" I asked again.

"Oh, it seems the poison tankers are arriving this afternoon. They're moving fast, the Government, because half of Oldhaven got burned down last night." He hesitated. "Do you mean to do what you're doing, Professor? I mean, stick around so that people can hate you and forget about hating one another?"

"It seemed a good idea," I admitted. "I'm not sure it's working, from what you say."

"Oh, it is," he said eagerly. "Things would be ten times worse without you to concentrate on. I think it's a great thing. I . . . I'm sorry we don't always seem to get on, Professor . . ." He was looking at me almost with awe.

"That's O.K., Tom," I said awkwardly. "We're all made differently; that's why we're having so much trouble with the Effect. Now, when are those tankers arriving? I want to see what happens. . . ."

"Around mid-afternoon. Ah . . . Are you thinking the same as me?"

"What's that?"

"I'm thinking they won't be able to poison the river," he said slowly. "I'm thinking the Minds will stop them, somehow. They've stopped everything else. And I'm thinking it's a pity if the Mind doesn't stop them, because they'll poison the sea forever, and all for nothing. . . ."

"Not entirely all for nothing, Tom. They'll kill the Minds and prevent the Effect, and save a lot of lives."

"But there's no need to kill the Minds," he said. "Not now that Mrs. Earnshaw and me have got it all worked out how to stop people fighting. I mean, we had a long talk, she and me, and we've got the answer to the whole thing."

He said it with the sublime, almost insolent confidence that characterized most of his actions and words. He said it as though, to him, it was nothing—a chance discovery tossed down like four aces, to be forgotten when the next hand began. I had been concerned about the Minds; he had the answer. O.K., so what next?"

"Hold it, Tom. Wait a minute." God, how I wanted to believe him. "What do you mean, you've got the answer?"

"As I said, there's nothing to worry about . . ." He grinned suddenly. "You're sitting on the answer right now, if you only knew it."

I seemed to be sitting on a pile of sacks, but I let him play it his way. "All right, tell me what you're talking about," I said mildly, my heart hammering.

"Well," he began, "I got to talking to old Mrs. Earnshaw about the problem of this trouble in the colony, and after a bit I got the idea she was pumping me, sort of. You know, as though she was trying to get to the bottom of me. It's not often folks are interested in what me and my pals are thinking," he said wistfully. "Mrs. Earnshaw, she's a good sort; makes you feel important. The Colony Committee's a load of crap!" he burst out suddenly. "They voted me on that Committee—the whole colony—and what happens? I find myself among a lot of old stick-in-the-muds who shut me up every time I open my mouth.

So what chance have I to put a new idea across? So I give up, don't I? I sit back and let them all get on with it."

"But Mrs. Earnshaw's not like that," I prompted him.

"No. She listens, and she's got ideas of her own. She was on about something you said, that we were going about dealing with the Mind the wrong way. It seems you said that instead of trying to get the Mind around to our way of thinking, we should adapt ourselves to it—like her scheme of saying just what she thinks. But that wasn't quite enough, she reckoned. It depends on folks being reasonable, and you can't always depend on that. So she asked me how I managed . . . She said my mind seemed calm, and that I didn't seem to want to fight, although she said she knew I was a natural troublemaker. That's true, too. I like to stir things up a bit. There's no sense in all of us getting in a rut."

"You stirred up some trouble for me, the other day."

"Don't get me wrong, Professor. You had it coming to you— if not from me, from someone else. They were all talking about you and Jane. If I hadn't brought it up when I did, someone else would have done it later, and backed it up with a knife, maybe. Not that I thought of that at the time. I reckon I just like to stir things up, as I said. Irresponsible, that's me."

"But now you've come up with something good," I reminded him.

"I'll say. Let me tell you a story, Professor. It won't take a minute . . . Years ago there was a man who bought a crap farm because he didn't know much about business, or farming either, but he wanted a place away from Premier City where he could keep a few animals and scratch a living. He was a harmless sort of fellow and easily taken in; besides, the figures looked good and they were all vouched for by the income tax people. So he bought the farm and pretty soon he found the land was no good and livestock were expensive, because anything good had to be bred from original Earth stock and there was a hell of a demand. It seemed he couldn't make money, and he wondered why, when the man he had bought the place from said it did so well, and had the figures to back it up.

"Then he found out. All the profits before had come from selling hardcore to the Government for the local road contracts. The roads had been finished a long time ago so hardly anybody needed hardcore any more. He felt he had been cheated. Maybe he should have looked further into the figures in the first place, but the fact remains he didn't, and it was too late now. He had a row with the tax department but it didn't do any good. They said they had only certified the profit figures; how it was made up wasn't their responsibility. So he was stuck with a crap farm which he couldn't sell, and which wouldn't make him a living.

"He told me all this one day. He told me how he couldn't pay his bills for fodder and how he wandered out into the fields one day feeling sick about the whole thing, with the Arcattle all thin and scraggy around him. He sat down by a pool and watched his Arcows drinking muddy water mixed with their own piss because he couldn't afford proper drainage and a main water supply. He said he sat there chewing on a root and thinking maybe he might jump into the shitty water and make an end to it. He sat there a long time and thought about it and gradually, he didn't know how, it seemed things weren't so bad after all . . .

"He went back to the house and thought a lot more, a hell of a lot more, because he knew that, by rights, he should be feeling low still, but he wasn't. He felt good enough to wonder why, and he was smart enough to guess that it had something to do with the root he was chewing. He had grubbed it up out of the ground near the pool. So he went back and grubbed up some more . . .

"He dried it and ground it in the mill, and he used it a lot after that, whenever things were getting too much for him. Later, years later, me and Jim and Bill came by to give him a hand with the shingles, and we got to talking about how folk in the colony got us down, and he said, try some of this. So we did, and we've been trying it ever since. It doesn't get a hold of you; you can leave it off whenever you want. It just makes you feel good for a while.

"I told him I thought it was great and there ought to be a market for it. And I found a market inland, and pretty soon old Farmer Blackstone was making enough money to get by. . . ."

He looked at me directly and there was no hint of apology in his expression. "I'm a pusher, Professor. That's what they call me, my contacts in town—a pusher. And what I do is against the law, and I could be put inside for it. I sell a drug on the black market. If you want to feel good, you go to the Club and have a beer or two, and if you have enough it makes you stupid, and you want to fight. And you may have a cigarette, and that doesn't really make you feel good, but you feel bad if you don't have one. You're hooked on the things, and they give you cancer. But the powder Farmer Blackstone ground from those roots just makes you feel peaceful, nothing more. Sure it's a drug, but it doesn't hook you like cigarettes, or make you stupid like beer. You stay just the same, but you're happy. You don't want to fight. You know exactly what you're doing all the time; it doesn't kid you into believing you're cleverer, or tougher, or anything. You can take it or leave it alone. Personally, I take it quite often. But I'm a criminal, a menace to society. Can you believe all this, Professor?"

"Yes, I can believe it, Tom," I said slowly. "I've wondered for a while why farm animals seem unaffected by the Mind. I've wondered why they didn't stampede at the emissions of fear, or plunge into the river as food for the blackfish. They're eating this plant all the time. They don't react to fear or violence."

"Like me, Jim and Bill," said Minty, grinning. He smacked the sack on which he was sitting. A puff of powder arose, brownish. "Care for a dose? Guaranteed no harmful after-effects. You may as well be the first. The main reason I came over here this morning was to pick up a sack to take to your place. Mrs. Earnshaw's finding it a strain, being truthful all the time. She wants to tell Miss Cotter exactly what she thinks of her, and then again she doesn't. Then we've got to try and push it around the colony."

Just for a few days, I thought . . . If we could persuade the colonists to take this stuff for just a few days until the danger was over . . . If Arthur was still here, we could arrange to move a supply inland for distribution. Just a pure happiness drug to give everyone a sensation of comfortable euphoria, sufficient for them to be able to ignore the Relay Effect . . . In fact, the Effect would cease to exist, because there would be no unpleasant thoughts to relay. Just goodwill, multiplied by the population of the colony. . . .

We returned to the house and I poured a glass of water. Minty dropped in a pinch of the brown powder. It didn't dissolve, but it was sufficiently fine to remain in suspension after stirring. With some trepidation, feeling like a secret addict, I drank. There was very little flavour, just a suggestion of sweetness. Minty drank a glass too. "Good health," he said, smacking his lips.

Soon, I began to feel pretty good.

SIXTEEN

Leaving me to my new enlightenment, Minty disappeared, and presently I heard a rumbling in the yard. I went out to see what was happening. He had brought a trolley, a four-wheeled affair with a long handle of the type they use on the quay to move crates of fish. He went into the shed, emerged staggering beneath the weight of a full sack, and off-loaded it onto the truck with a thud. Watching him, I experienced a surge of fellowship towards the youth. I was aware that this feeling was due in part to the drug I had taken, but this did not alter the fact that he was working hard for the common good. I seemed to have gained a new insight. I began to wonder just how many of Minty's difficulties were of his own seeking; it was apparent that his normal air of dissatisfaction and antipathy were largely due to his environment. Riverside had been in pretty much of a rut for a long time—since the sub-colony was founded, in fact. It must be frustrating for a moderately intelligent person who wanted to change things.

I wondered, for the first time, how much success he and Mrs. Earnshaw would have in their effort to persuade the colonists to use the drug. . . .

"Hold it, Tom!" I called. "I'll give you a hand to the top of the ridge."

We took the truck handle and, side by side, began to trundle it out of the yard. As we passed through the gate and into the long field that runs up to the crest of the ridge, the going became heavy. The small wheels, designed for the hard road surface, were constantly bogging down or wedging against the sharp rocks projecting from the grass. Minty grinned at me briefly, sweat pouring down his forehead. Then he stopped suddenly.

"Look!" He pointed down to the right, where the road wound among the agricultural land. A hovercar was moving inland, nearing the junction with the short farm road. It was Arthur's car; I could see four people inside. The team was pulling out. I shouted and waved; they were about two hundred yards below us and moving slowly, presumably looking out for me. Suddenly they stopped, and I saw a hand acknowledge my signalling. They moved off again, turned left, and hissed down the road to the farm, raising a cloud of dust from the loose surface.

"Come on, Tom," I said. "We'll leave the truck here for the time being. Let's go and see what Arthur's got to tell us."

We met them in the farmyard, four dejected men standing around the grounded car.

"Hello there, Mark," Arthur greeted me heavily. "It's good to see you're all right. We were worried about you, but there seemed to be nothing we could do."

"You're leaving?" I asked.

They glanced at each other sheepishly. "Reckon so," admitted Don McCabe. "We've done all we can, and we don't fancy hanging round just to see a few million gallons of poison pumped into the river. It's not my idea of entertainment. We've been recalled, so we're getting out right away. Let's face it, we've failed."

"Do you really think the Minds will let them poison the river?" I asked. "They seem pretty adept at defending themselves."

"How are they going to stop them?" Arthur retorted bitterly. I sensed utter defeat from the minds of the team.

"I don't know," I confessed. "But then, there are a lot of things I don't know about the Minds."

Arthur was regarding me narrowly. "What the hell's got into you?" he asked suddenly. There was a realization in his thoughts, a surprised interest overlying the misery. "You're not scared any more, are you? Neither for yourself, or for the colony . . . You seem . . . happy. So does this lad here." Incredulity showed on his face. "Are you on to something? Do you know something we don't?"

"Could be," I said.

Briefly I described the events of the past few hours and my discussion with Minty. I told them about Blackstone and his illegal source of income. Finally I took them into the small dome and showed them the sacks of powder. At first, I don't think they believed us, but there was the evidence of our own minds as proof. I decided that a demonstration would be in order, so we went into the house, where each member of the team sampled the drug with an expression of deep mistrust, like a man tasting home-made wine.

It was the first time I had experienced, from an observer's standpoint, the extraordinary changes in a person's thought processes after he had taken this drug. The four men stood around the table, watching each other nervously, scrutinizing one another's faces as though expecting a werewolf transformation. I could read the fear in their minds—the residue of fear following their flight from the colony, which I knew was more enforced than they had given me to understand. Apparently, as my associates, they were coming under fire from the private colonists, and Don McCabe had already been goaded into a fight. I saw the strain there, the frustration of working long hours in a hostile environment only to be thwarted at each turn by an intelligence too alien to allow normal methods of psychiatric study. I saw the defeat and the despondency.

I saw all this—their minds were open to me but, under the soothing effect of the drug I had taken, their emotions did not influence my own. And I saw the fear and the strain and the defeat gradually abating as the drug entered their bloodstreams and circulated in their brains. It was fantastic—almost religious, a purification ceremony.

Don McCabe was looking at me in wonder. "I feel so good, Mark," he whispered. "I feel great suddenly, just like that. It's amazing!"

Pendlebury was not a man to believe the evidence of his own mind. I caught a flash of cynicism in his thoughts. "I feel great after a beer or two," he said. "How can you be sure this isn't the same thing?"

"I can't explain it," I told him. "But it's true, all the same. This is a different effect from alcohol. I first noticed it some time ago when I was talking to Tom Minty here. He's been on the drug for a long time. This drug doesn't dull the mind like alcohol. You're still perfectly alert and your reactions are unimpaired. It doesn't even block off the emissions of people around you. But the sense of well-being is so deep-seated that you're able to ignore the fear and hate emissions relayed to you, while still being aware of their existence. Basically, other people's thoughts will not affect you; neither will your own resultant thoughts contribute to the Relay Effect. So far as I can tell, this is the complete answer."

Arthur said slowly: "We must put this across to the Government. The drug must be distributed around the coastal areas at once. I take it you're going to look after the colony?"

"If they'll let us. We're relying on Mrs. Earnshaw to put it across to them."

"I'll get an announcement put over the radio. I'll call from the next town and get them to stop the tankers, if there's time." His manner became urgent as he went on. "God, we'll have to move fast. We've got to persuade the Arcadian Council to do a complete re-think, then act immediately."

"We'll load your car with as many sacks as it'll take," I said.

"Right. Let's get going, then."

The side panels drooped against the ground by the time the car was loaded; then Arthur and the others got in and drove off rapidly.

"O.K., Professor," said Minty. "Let's get that truck up the hill. I'll leave you at the top. Better if you don't let yourself be seen around the colony until everybody's good and high."

At the hilltop I sat down in the scrub. Minty stood watching the colony.

"Doesn't seem to be much happening," he observed. "Still, if you stay up here I'll take the truck down. It'll be easy enough from now on. Mrs. Earnshaw will be organizing her meeting right now, I expect . . ." He paused awkwardly. "Would you like me to send Jane up here?"

"Thanks a lot," I said.

"Fine. She can give you the latest news. And I'll tell everyone that me and the lads are taking care of Blackstone's animals. That way nobody's going to come bothering you later."

I watched as he towed the truck down the slope, then turned it around and ran behind as the grade steepened, braking frantically with his heels as it threatened to get out of control. Soon he reached level ground, veered right, trudged through the meadow and, with difficulty, up the hump and over the bridge. Jim Spark and Bill Yong emerged from the ships' chandler's on the quay and hurried to meet him. There was a short conversation, then the three of them dragged the truck up the steep hill to the upper colony. Soon they disappeared from sight around the corner.

I waited impatiently for about two hours, watching the opposite hillside. Then at last Jane appeared in the distance and began to descend the street. Five minutes later she dropped to the ground beside me, out of breath.

"Sorry I was such a long time," she apologized. "We've been trying to sort things out for the meeting. Did you see anyone following me?"

"No." I laughed. I was glad to see her again. "You make it sound like a spy thriller," I said.

"It's serious, Mark," she replied. "There's a terrific amount of ill-feeling against you among the private colonists. It's building up all the time. It's only the fact of the tankers arriving soon that's stopped them from coming after you already."

"What about my own men?" I asked. "Surely I must have the support of the Station."

"Didn't you know?" She regarded me with slight embarrassment. "They pulled out this morning."

"What!"

"It hasn't given a very good impression, Mark," she said seriously. "The Government recalled them—you too, of course—and they all left just before dawn in the Research Centre trucks."

I thought for a moment. "I suppose it's better this way. We've had them confined to their units in any case, just in the event that the private colonists ganged up on them as convenient scapegoats."

"The private colonists are saying that the Government's looked after its own people and left everyone else to die."

"There's a grain of truth in that too," I said. "But at least it helps to unite them."

"They're having a meeting."

"Mrs. Earnshaw's meeting?"

"No. They've got one of their own, a sort of war council. They're discussing you, and the business of poisoning the sea. They blame you for that, too."

"What! Damn it, I've been against the poisoning from the start!"

"Just try to tell them that now. I know, I've tried myself. You don't realize what it's like, Mark. They all seem to have gone mad. They won't listen to any sort of reason at all. I've been on Tom Minty's drug for a while. I had some last night after we'd talked it over, but I could still sense this . . . feeling in the air." She shivered suddenly. "A sort of communal madness. A mass hysteria—the air's so thick with hate and stupidity they couldn't think straight if they wanted to. They say you're a marine biologist, so you must have had the idea of the poison and suggested it to Arthur, who passed it on to the Government."

"But it doesn't make sense," I protested. "If they're that stupid, then surely all they would want to do would be to get rid of the Minds by the quickest means and damn the consequences. They ought to welcome the poison."

"They don't know what they want. The horrible thing is, they seem almost to revel in the situation. They enjoy the hate; they don't want it to be diminished. It's like a football match my father once took me to see in Oldhaven. I didn't understand much about it at the time, but apparently it was an important game. The home crowd yelled murder at the opposition as soon as they took the field. It went on right through the game, deafening, a solid roar of hate. I couldn't understand it. The opposition were just men, like the home team. In fact, I suppose they were better men, because they won. I looked around at one point to ask my father what he had against these poor men, then I looked away again quickly. Because his face was all twisted up with hate, just like the rest of them. Afterwards he said he'd thoroughly enjoyed the game, in spite of his team losing. I asked him why he didn't cheer his own team on, instead of yelling at the opposition. He said something about it being because his team were losing; and besides, the opposition were committing a lot of fouls.

"But for over an hour I'd seen a huge crowd hating somebody just for the fun of it, and I didn't like that. That's what it's like in the colony now. Nothing will distract them from hating you, because that's the way they want it. The sea's going to be poisoned? Right, so it's your fault. Who else is there?"

I looked at her as she lay beside me in sweater and jeans and I knew that the deaths and physical injuries would not be the only tragedies of the Relay Effect. From now on, at least until the next generation, a person would never look at his neighbour in quite the same way. . . .

And I wondered again about the power of the Minds. "Jane," I said, "The Minds know the poison is coming. They've reached a stage of development where they can anticipate danger by analysing the thoughts they relay. Look at how they dealt with Phipps and the others in the boat . . . Now, what can we do about it? Otherwise, what will the colony do about it?"

She regarded me thoughtfully. "I see what you mean . . . The way I think of it, it's possible that this whole business of identifying you with the Government has been prompted by the Minds themselves. . . ."

"In which case," I surmised, "the Minds will use the colonists to avert the danger, just like they use the blackfish. They've achieved a direct influence on people. I think it's possible we're going to see some sort of battle around the tanker . . ." I stood up. "Come on. We've got to intercept the truck. We've got to try to stop them from getting as far as the colony."

We stood together on the inland road, and much later we heard the distant roar of a heavy vehicle approaching. Soon we could see it across the tops of the fences, a huge petrol hover-tanker with black and yellow markings. It rounded the bend and headed towards us, turbine racing as the driver put on speed for the hill. We waved urgently. I stepped into the middle of the road. The tanker pulled up and subsided with a hiss of exhausted air from the side.

"Want to get yourself killed?" The driver leaned out, glaring.

There were three men in the cab. The one in the middle looked like some sort of official. I addressed him.

"There's been a change of plan," I told him. "You don't need to use this stuff. You can reverse up the road and go back." I pointed to the farm track, some twenty yards away.

The official gazed at me sceptically. "We've been warned about this sort of thing," he said. "They told us there might be people trying to stop us. They said we should take no notice and drive on . . . Out of the way then! Get moving, George!" He addressed the driver.

"Wait!" Jane was beside me. "He's telling the truth! They've got a new drug . . ." She looked at me desperately, conscious of how implausible it sounded. "How can we convince them, Mark?"

"You can't." The driver blipped his throttle. "I should step aside if I were you. I wouldn't want you to get hurt."

Suddenly I had an idea. "Just give us a ride to the top of the hill," I said. "No further. I want to show you something."

They looked at me doubtfully. "O.K.," the official said at last. "If you ask me," he remarked as we squeezed into the cab, "there's something strange about this whole thing. Tipping all this poison into the sea. It seems to me it's going to do a lot of harm. I don't know what this Effect is that they're all talking about, but this seems a pretty drastic action to take."

"So you've never experienced the Effect," I said. "Well, now's your chance." We were approaching the hilltop, turbine screaming. "Just try opening your mind," I advised him. "Make it blank. Let the thoughts come in."

We were in sight of the colony. A huge crowd had gathered near the bridge.

The tanker pulled up. The crew sat for a moment, their eyes wide in wonder, and then fear. . . .

"I'm scared," remarked the official nervously. "Those people down there, they scare me. Why's that?" It was very quiet in the cab; the driver had stopped the turbine and we sat still, waiting as the Effect built up.

"They've seen us," said the driver suddenly. "They want to kill us. I know they do. They're all looking this way. I can tell. they're going to drag us out and kill us!" His voice had risen to a shout of panic. He started the turbine and rammed the reverse thrust. "I'm getting out of here!" he yelled as the vehicle rose from the road. The tanker roared backwards, dust flew, he twisted around, juggling with the wheel. . . .

We were lucky in Riverside that day. The full story emerged later. In seven coastal sub-colonies, the tankers had actually arrived before the occupants became aware of the hostility around them. Then suddenly the Effect had reached them and they had accelerated, screaming through the narrow street pursued by a murderous mob, mowing down pedestrians as they went.

And in three colonies the trucks had stopped short of the sea.

The crews had got out and, moving like zombies, had pumped the contents of their tanks into the fresh-water reservoirs. . . .

SEVENTEEN

We didn't find that out until a day or two later, when the combination of rumour and guarded radio reports could be pieced together to make some sort of picture. That afternoon, we thought we had done rather well; and Jane and I were congratulating ourselves as we left the tanker and its terrified occupants at the junction with the farm road. We had averted a tragedy that would undoubtedly have involved considerable loss of life.

So we walked along the track to the farm and gradually became aware of a constraint between us. We walked a little apart. Glancing at Jane, I saw that her head was down and she was examining the dusty road as she scuffed her feet along childishly. There was an unspoken suggestion in the minds of each of us, and neither wanted to get it into the open. Mrs. Earnshaw might have solved our problem, but she was doubtless preparing for her meeting. In any case, the last thing I wanted was to be completely frank with Jane at that moment.

But I knew her, and I knew that sooner or later she would force the issue.

"What's it like at the farm?" she asked brightly. "I've never been there before."

"Old, and a bit dirty," I said. "It needs a complete renovation. You know what a place gets like when a man lives by himself."

"I'd noticed." She grinned. and I could have kicked myself. She moved closer to me as we walked and put her arm through mine. "Never mind, old man, I'll help you clean it up. I can't have you living in squalour while you're on the run, can I?"

"What about Mrs. Earnshaw's meeting?" I asked desperately. "You ought to be there. She'll need backing up. I was thinking I might try to get there myself, somehow. Inconspicuously, of course."

She was silent for a moment. Then she said, in a small voice: "Do you really want me to go back to the colony, Mark?"

"There's a lot happening," I said. "We can't just think of ourselves. We've got to keep in touch."

"But everything will be all right now," she insisted. "All she's got to do is tell them to take a dose of Tom Minty's drug, and the whole problem's solved. It's simple. And probably by morning they'll have given it out over the radio and made it legal. That'll take care of any objectors."

"I'm not so sure of that," I said.

She stopped suddenly, still holding my arm, swinging me around to face her. She looked straight at me and I was forced to drop my eyes. Her face was pink. "This is the second time, Mark," she said quietly. "You dodged the issue at the house the other night. You're doing it again. By all that's reasonable, I should stay with you at this farm. You know I don't need to go back. But you don't want me around."

"I do, Jane," I found myself saying before I could prevent it.

"How do I know that?" she cried furiously. She stood away from me. "I can't understand you, Mark. I thought the other night that perhaps you loved me. I more or less admitted I loved you, and I reckon I made no end of a fool of myself. Because there's something else, isn't there? Something that you won't tell anyone about, something that comes between you and me." She gazed into my face, searching and I felt her mind touching mine, probing. I tried to discipline my thoughts, but it was useless. Her eyes widened.

"It's Sheila!" she exclaimed. "My God, it's Sheila still, after she's been dead six months." The callousness of her words struck her, and her voice softened suddenly. "I'm sorry, Mark. I shouldn't have said that. Six months is a very short time . . . Do you . . . Do you think you'll ever forget her enough to love me?" She was speaking quietly, almost to herself. "We did look a lot alike, but her hair was nicer than mine. Mrs. Earnshaw was wrong. You do see her every time you look at me, and it gives you some sort of guilt complex. Look at me now, Mark. Look at me and be honest with yourself."

Dumbly, I looked into her eyes.

She flinched and looked away. "You hate her, Mark," she muttered in bewilderment. "You loved her and something terrible happened, and now you hate her memory; and that's why you're scared to love me, because you can't help identifying us together. Mark, you're wrong. Whatever you think Sheila did, you're wrong. I know she loved you, because she used to tell me everything. I'd have known if there was someone else . . . You think there was someone else, don't you?" She was staring at the ground but her thoughts were probing mine ruthlessly. "The night she was killed, you've got some reason for thinking she met a lover by Anchor Pool. You can't understand why she was out there all alone at night. You've found something to suggest that she was . . . familiar with someone, that they . . ."

She straightened up and looked at me squarely. "Well, I ought to hate you for thinking that about my sister, Mark, but I don't. I feel sorry for you because I know you're wrong and one day you're going to feel damned ashamed. Goodbye."

I watched her walk quickly back along the road and one part of my mind was thinking it was a good exit line, and the other part was crying.

The colony was silent as I crept up the hill towards the Recreation Dome; the few street lights were on, and I flitted from shadow to shadow like a ham actor in a 3-V thriller. Most of the units were in darkness. As I approached the dome I saw a few people standing in the doorway, and behind them, in the light through the open door, the backs of a large seated assembly. The meeting was about to commence. I slipped through a gate some thirty yards short of the dome and picked my way through a tangle of thorns and shrubs to the far side of the building, where a curving row of lighted windows promised a good view of the proceedings. Sidling up to the window nearest the platform end of the dome, I peered in cautiously.

The window was slightly open at the bottom, and the voices came to me clearly. Seated on the platform were Mrs. Earnshaw, Tom Minty, Bill Yong, Jim Spark, Jane and, inevitably, the Reverend E. L. Blood. Mrs. Earnshaw rose to her feet; apparently the Reverend's opening address was over. I had missed it. I was not conscious of any regret.

I was, however, conscious of an emanation of restlessness from the audience. Mrs. Earnshaw had not started yet, but feet were shuffling and there was scattered coughing and trumpeting into handkerchiefs. It was possible that this was due to the Reverend's oration, but I doubted it. Something else was affecting the audience; they were going to prove difficult to handle. It came to me gradually—a general desire to be on the move, to start running across the fields mindlessly, like a terrestrial lemming. It was a variation of the emanations I had detected when I was being pursued, but now the suggestion of hunting was not accompanied by any specific quarry image. It was disturbing. . . .

"Ladies and Gentlemen, I'll keep it brief." Mrs. Earnshaw had commenced; she had also correctly judged the mood of her audience. There was a noticeable feeling of relief. "Today we witnessed an ill-advised attempt to poison our water. Fortunately the truck involved turned back on seeing the strength of the opposition. I think we can fairly say that a victory was won."

She was playing it well, praising them, putting herself at one with her audience. There was a murmur of self-approbation. The enemy had been fought off. The colony was unspoiled. I could feel it myself, strong in their thoughts. Then the disquieting idea occurred to me. Who, exactly, did they think the enemy was? Had they completely forgotten the danger from the Minds? I hoped Mrs. Earnshaw would not take her present line too far. . . .

She didn't. "But we must not forget the fundamental peril," she continued immediately. "That is, the Relay Effect caused by the Minds in the estuary. The Government, as is the way of such bodies, has failed to provide an adequate solution. It is tragic that, when faced with a situation such as this, they can only think of destruction—and destruction on such an indiscriminate scale that it would endanger our livelihood forever!" She paused for a round of applause and, I was relieved to hear, got it.

"We of Riverside could have told them that their method was certain to prove abortive. In our small way we have tried to deal with the Minds, with tragic results, as we know to our cost. But we have learned from these mistakes. We are still learning. And now, I think I can safely say that every person here is aware that tactics must be changed. It is the old story. In order to survive in this changed environment, we must adapt ourselves."

I sensed the restlessness growing again. There was a single, loud bark of laughter from young Paul Blake. . . .

Mrs. Earnshaw hurried on. "For a short while, until the danger is past, we must adapt. You might ask: How?" (At this point someone did ask how, loudly and derisively.) "I will tell you." She thumped the sack before her and a little brown cloud arose. "The answer is here!"

Amid a growing murmuring and shuffling she described briefly the discovery of the drug and its effect on the thought processes. She tried hard, she shouted, she pleaded . . . She got nowhere. She had lost her audience, inexplicably.

I was scared. I stood by that window sweating, unable to understand what was gong wrong. The emanations from the crowd were not hostile; there was no feeling of violence. They were cynical, indifferent to the extent that it became obvious they had no intention even of trying the drug. It was a weird kind of active apathy. It was there, in the atmosphere, a blunt refusal to know or care what happened next. . . .

It was the Minds. It must be the Minds. They were affecting the reasoning power of the audience, picking up the logical input from Mrs. Earnshaw and relaying it back scrambled and over-laid with scepticism. I could feel it myself. The Minds did not want anybody to use the drug. The Minds had ideas of their own. The Minds did not want to relinquish control. . . .

Mrs. Earnshaw was sitting down. She exchanged alarmed glances with Jane and Minty and his friends. The Reverend Blood stood, clearing his throat in the sudden silence.

"Well, now," he began. "I think we all agree that Mrs. Earnshaw has an interesting idea. I'm sure we all agree also that it's unwise to get carried away by it, by this panacea which she has produced so opportunely. For what do we know of this drug, my friends? Has it been analysed? What does anyone know? Simply what we have been told. And what are we told? That it makes Tom Minty feel good. Well, now," he laughed indulgently, "we'll have to do better than that, Mrs. Earnshaw. We all know young Tom, and there are some of us who also know, to our cost, that he sometimes feels good. I remember he and his friends feeling good two months ago when they smashed a stained-glass window in our church, in an excess of youthful high spirits. There have been other such instances of vandalism around the colony. I'm not accusing anyone, mind you—but it's only fair to say that we all have our ideas as to the culprits. Not that it's necessarily their fault. I say in fairness that the blame lies with each one of us here, for we are the adults who allow these children access to drugs which poison their minds just as surely as the Government would have poisoned our waters."

There was an outburst of tumultuous applause, fortified by foot stamping. The normally ineffectual Reverend was delivering the oration of his life. He was possessed. . . .

Mrs. Earnshaw was on her feet shouting: "Are these your own ideas, Blood? Or do they come from another source—the estuary, maybe? Whose mind is poisoned, for God's sake?"

In the uproar that followed the Reverend could be seen shaking his head sadly. He held up his hand. "Mrs. Earnshaw," he said as the audience quieted, "I will forgive you for that, because I realize you are not yourself. You have been taken in by the young man who sits with us on the platform—and you are not the first. We all know he can be persuasive when he likes; remember, we voted him onto the Colony Committee . . . But I think that I must regretfully call this meeting to an end. We've all heard what you've said, and we've listened patiently. Now we must go to our homes. Tonight I suggest that, each of us in his own way, we pray . . . For ourselves and our people around the coast, for those misguided people you see on the platform—"

He was looking directly at me as I stood outside the window; I knew too late that I had moved into the light. I caught a glint of unspeakable malice in his eyes as I moved back. . . .

"—and most of all, for Professor Mark Swindon, whose crimes I do not need to enumerate, but who has himself attended this meeting in sly fashion, lacking the courage to . . ."

I didn't hear any more because I was running, stumbling over shrubs in my path, vaulting the wall, racing down the street in the glare of the lamps. . . .

Behind me, I heard the animal roar of pursuit.

They were close behind me and they stayed close all the way to the point, yet there did not seem to be the same urgency in the chase. The emanations were there, the urge to kill, but it was moderated, almost as if I had become a habit which bored them. I climbed down the hoist cable and dropped to the shingle beach, pushed the rowboat out, jumped in and pulled for *Carousel*. Soon I saw them silhouetted against the sky at the cliff-top. There were only about twenty, shouting after me; and soon they drifted away.

I climbed on board *Carousel* and switched on the battery lamp. I tried to work it out. On the previous occasion when the mob had been after me, I had no doubt that their urge to kill had been aggravated by my own fear coming back to them strongly. Now that I had Minty's drug, that stimulus would be removed. Nevertheless I was sure that there was some other factor. It was almost as though the Relay Effect was fading. As though the growing powers of direct control were rendering it obsolete.

I cooked myself some bacon and eggs in the tiny galley while I worked on the problem, then returned to the cockpit and turned out the light. It was always possible that my pursuers, knowing there was only one dinghy at the point, had returned to the colony and were motoring down the estuary to resume the chase. I listened carefully but could hear nothing other than the lapping of water and the occasional splash of a leaping fatty. As my eyes became accustomed to the darkness I could make out the gaps between the headlands at the estuary mouth. Looking up, I saw the rare, incredible sight of the clouds parting to reveal the six moons of Arcadia glowing, closely grouped, in the night sky. They formed the approximate shape of a boot— Beth, Daleth and Vau in the leg; the foot angling away and consisting of Aleph, Gimel and He. The water now shone silver, and the cliffs were a jagged contrast of black and white. Like stars scattered over the sea were the feeding mewlers, and in the dark distance the huge silver form of a scoopbill was winging lazily eastward. The sight was unutterably beautiful, and I wished Jane had been with me in that boat. . . .

I opened my mind in what had now become the accustomed manner and felt around for emanations. There were none. The confused whisper of thoughts from the colony was gone. Indeed, the only impression I gained was of a strange gladness, as though I, or somebody, was being thanked for a great service given.

I wondered for a moment if the Minds had died—if, their duty now complete and their spawn flooding out to the oceans, they were at this moment disintegrating, their powers fading.

Then I remembered my certainty that the rejection of Mrs. Earnshaw at the meeting was inspired by an outside source. This was proof that the Minds were still active, at the height of their powers. They were not finished with us yet. . . .

The scoopbill had turned inland; it veered and flew low over the boat with a whining of pinions, heading for the estuary. Near the headland it plunged into the water in a silver cascade of spray. I regarded the point where it disappeared with interest; I had never seen a scoopbill dive before. It did not re-emerge. . . .

I left the cockpit and went forward to ensure that the mooring chain was secure, yet tied in a fashion to allow a quick getaway if necessary. Satisfied, I started back, when another silver splash caught my eye. I leaned over the side of the boat, peering into the water. The surface was littered with white feathers, drifting past the hull of *Carousel*. Deeper below the surface, there was something else. . . .

The sea was alive with fatties, dark shapes swimming in the direction of the estuary. Thousands of them—they must have comprised the entire population of my pens along the coast. At first I thought they must be impelled by hunger. Due to the various problems, I doubted whether Perce had been able to feed them regularly; so they had escaped with the high tide, swimming over the tops of the nets. I was dismayed; it would take months, years even, to restock the pens and set up the various experiments again. Junkers dived among them, picking off the smaller fish with raucous screams.

Then it dawned on me—they were swimming directly to their death in the estuary. As I watched, I saw sparkling swirls in the water near the headland as the teeming blackfish struck, and once again I was aware of the emanation of gratitude. . . .

And once more I was reminded of the terrestrial lemming.

EIGHTEEN

The next morning set the pattern that I was to follow for several days. Around mid-morning there would be a shout from the cliff-top and I would see Perce Walters waving to me. I would row ashore in the dinghy and meet him on the beach; he would have brought food and drink, together with news from the front.

It seemed that Mrs. Earnshaw's talk had not been a total failure, despite the opposition led by the Reverend Blood. At that time there had been seven people using the drug, namely Jane, Mrs. Earnshaw, Miss Cotter (reluctantly), Minty, Yong, Spark, and myself. As a result of the lecture another four had approached Mrs. Earnshaw and received their supply, these being Perce Walters and his mother Annie of the erotic fears, John Talbot of the Social Club (who had not left with the rest of the Station staff) and, more surprisingly, Alan Phipps. This latter convert was influenced, I think, by the death of his father in the dynamite incident. So now there were eleven of us against the colony, I said to Perce two days later.

He informed me that this was not strictly true. The whole population had calmed down and, apart from the refusal to use the drug, was behaving in a commendably rational manner. There had been no further fighting, riots or arson. When my pursuers had returned home two nights ago, the reaction to the news of my escape was phlegmatic. As Perce put it, the heat seemed to be off me. There had been no suggestion of sending a posse down river to round me up.

Indeed, there had been no suggestion of anything, which Perce found disturbing.

"They seem to be back to normal, Professor," he said one day. "Only more so, if you get my meaning. It's as though they've forgotten everything that's happened this past week or two.

They don't talk about the Minds and they don't talk about the folk who died. It seemed to come on quite suddenly, after that meeting. I can't get any sense out of them. They've shut the whole business out of their minds."

"Even the Reverend Blood?"

"Him particularly. He gets great crowds at his church. Nearly the whole colony attends every evening. I went the other night, though I'm not one for that kind of thing. I couldn't see what the attraction was. Everyone sat there quiet while the Reverend went on in his usual style. There seemed to be nothing different. He never mentioned the Minds."

"Just what did he say? We've come through a time of great trial, and general terms like that?"

"No. Nothing like that. He kept on about the Cosmic Purpose, or some such thing. I didn't like it much, because if I believe in anything at all, it's that a man is here to do his best. But the flock lapped it up."

There was a dread at the corner of my mind—something I couldn't quite pin down, but it nagged at my thoughts like an early cancer. "What did he mean by Cosmic Purpose, Perce?"

"I'm not quite sure, but it seemed he was saying we were all part of an overall Plan. He said this was a good thing and we should all realize it and not try to fight it. It showed we were not alone. God made all creatures, he said. He told us how wrong they used to be on Earth when they said that only men had souls. He said how exploration had found thinking beings on other planets who were better than us in some ways." Perce paused, scratching his head. "What he said was quite true in a sense, but it was the way he put it. Sort of slanted . . . Pessimistic. It was almost as if he was telling us to . . . drift along, like, not to fight things, not even to use the brains we've got. Just to surrender to this Cosmic Plan of his."

"And you say the congregation went along with this?"

"Oh, yes. It's funny the way they're acting, as though they're the ones who are drugged, not us. They move and think like zombies."

Like zombies . . . I remembered the report I'd heard of the tanker that had stopped short of the town and pumped poison into the reservoir. The crew, it was said, moved like zombies. . . .

I had a portable radio on *Carousel* and I listened to the news each day. The announcers gave the impression of cautious optimism; apparently all along the coast things had quietened down, although they were at pains to impress upon the population that the danger was not yet past. In particular, they urged people to take their daily dose of Immunol, as they had christened Blackstone's drug. From the tone of veiled menace in which the request was couched, I gathered that a large section of the population had refused the drug. . . .

I spent most of my time puzzling over the new situation in the colony. In an effort to lend some sense to the sequence of events. I catalogued the effects of the Minds in chronological order.

First, The colony had become aware of the Relay Effect. At first I had thought this was an accidental by-product of the Mind's powers, but now I wasn't so sure. I tried to imagine a newly-born Mind, powerless apart from its instinct for self-defence, which it exercised through direct control of the blackfish. It became apparent that I was putting events in the wrong order. The Relay Effect must have come first. This was the instinctive power, born with the Mind, which required no experience or intelligence to operate. It had evolved as a simple means of stimulating the natural viciousness of the blackfish, thus protecting the Mind from the outset.

Then, second, as the Mind developed it began to exercise direct control in such a manner that it could mass the blackfish, deploy them, and organize attacks whenever it felt itself in danger. Thus it had dealt with the plankton fishermen.

Three. With further development came the realization that it was not the sole intelligent inhabitant of the area. It began to monitor the random thoughts of the human beings around it. Learning all the time, collating, it began to make sense of what it heard, and to pick out the signals that directly concerned it as an entity.

Four. The Mind progressed to a stage where it could act on information received. At first its powers were crude—a mere negation, but effective nevertheless. It read the danger in Officer Clarke's mind, recognized it to be centred on the stick of explosive in his hand and, for the first time, exercised a modicum of control over an intelligent being. It leeched his motor senses; it prevented him from relaxing the muscles of his hand. And it knew, now, that Man was an enemy. . . .

Five. The Mind was not fully developed; control over Man's intelligence had progressed to active compulsion where necessary for defence. Hence the organized bands gathered together to prevent the Government's poison project and the incidents of unplanned poisoning of water supplies.

Six. And here I paused. What was the next stage? The Relay Effect was fading. It was not now strictly necessary—direct compulsion had been achieved. What had the Minds in view? Their defence was impregnable and, I was forced to admit, they had always acted in self-defence. Added to this, their short life was coming to an end. Why, then, this new influence on the colony? Why the refusal to allow the population to take the drug? Perhaps they had discovered that the drug inhibited their control as well as preventing the Relay Effect. But why promote this general apathy?

I gave up. I suppose I thought that the Minds were still scared of us and were not prepared to allow any change in the status quo that might diminish their influence. It was perfectly feasible. We had proved ourselves dangerous in the past and might do so again, given the chance.

But the Mind was intelligent and experienced now, or so we must suppose. Surely it must realize that Man only rebelled against the Relay Effect because of the danger to himself. And now this Effect was fading, becoming obsolete. The Minds *must* know that the reasons for Man's enmity had passed—that, given the chance, he would now allow the birth cycle of the plankton to proceed unhindered, for his own benefit. . . .

I put all this to Mrs. Earnshaw when she arrived with Perce one morning. Her reaction was typical; for all I knew then, it might have been correct.

"The Minds are bitchy," she said forcefully. "They've had so much trouble with us that they've got vindictive. They're going to make things awkward for us right up to the day they all die. Can you blame them? We're the intruders, after all. They've been here for thousands of years. . . ."

I asked her about the Relay Effect.

"It's fading," she told me. "There's just this feeling of . . . I don't know, a sort of contentment. So strong that nobody does any work. A sense of satisfaction and gratitude, obviously coming direct from the Minds. What they're grateful for, God only knows. . . ."

"Do you think it's safe for me to come back?" I asked. "I'm not happy about things. It seems to me that the Minds must have something up their sleeves, so to speak. They've got a good reason for wanting to maintain control. For God's sake, don't stop taking the drug . . . I think I ought to be around, in case something starts up again."

"Stay right here," she advised me firmly. "There's nothing you can do in Riverside. Everything's quiet, yes; but they've got this religious mania, and it would only take a word from Blood to turn it against you. I've got so that I mistrust *any* new manifestation, no matter how harmless it seems. They're eating out of Blood's hand."

"What about Jane," I asked at last.

"She'll be all right . . ." Mrs. Earnshaw glanced at me sharply. "You've done something to upset her, haven't you? She came home crying that evening when the tanker came, and she's been very quiet ever since. I can't get her to come here with me. You're a bastard, Mark, upsetting a nice girl like that. What did you do to her?"

"I didn't do anything," I protested.

"Maybe you should have," she replied. "Young Phipps is sniffing round her again," she added meaningfully. "He's one of us now. He's on the drug."

"I'm not worried about Alan Phipps," I said too loudly.

She looked at me for a long time. "I can't tell what you're thinking," she said at last. "Those days are passing, thank God. But if there's something that's come between you and Jane, you ought to clear it up quickly. There's something . . . desperate about her. Quiet and desperate. I keep an eye on her, but I can't be there all the time. I may be wrong, but I get the idea she's working herself up to something. I don't know what. . . ."

Naturally I was concerned by Mrs. Earnshaw's remarks, but there didn't seem to be a lot I could do. If Jane didn't want to see me, I could hardly force myself on her. After rowing Mrs. Earnshaw back to the beach and watching her hoisted, undignified, to the cliff-top by Perce, I returned to *Carousel* and cast off. I was becoming tired of staying in one place all the time; I thought I would go along the coast a short distance and inspect the fish pens.

It was, of course, low tide when I arrived, so I was not able to motor over the top of the nets. I made a circuit of the perimeter, however, close to the buoys, travelling slowly and peering over the side. During my whole examination of the pens I didn't see one fatty. They had all departed in that mass exodus to the estuary. Depressed, I turned around and headed back. I cruised among the trawlers, inspecting the anchor chains. Everything was in order. Then I made for the headland, a quarter of a mile away.

The tide was still falling as *Carousel* sliced through the murky water, and again I hung over the side, examining the suspended mud and floating debris for signs of the tiny shrimp-like plankton. I saw a few but nothing like the countless billions that had been in evidence in the previous weeks. Obviously the breeding cycle was coming to an end, and the Minds would soon, presumably, die. Encouraged by this, I returned to the mooring off the point, tied up and had a beer, feeling more optimistic. In a day or so I would be able to return home and, I hoped, everything would be back to normal again. . . .

In those few quiet days on *Carousel* I was able to think more objectively about Jane and the barrier in our relationship. I was able to admit to myself that I had been unfair to her, that my ambiguous memories of Sheila had created an impossible situation so far as she was concerned. I resolved to try and forget the whole terrible episode of Sheila's death and make a fresh start, if Jane would let me. Having decided this, I found it very difficult to remain on the boat. . . .

Then one morning a deputation arrived.

I saw them waving from the cliff-top and my heart leaped. Surely that was Jane? I jumped into the dinghy and rowed rapidly for the shore, by which time they had reached the beach —Perce, Mrs. Earnshaw, John Talbot, Alan Phipps, and Jane. We exchanged greetings but my eyes were on Jane; she, however, was looking everywhere but at me.

"Something's happened," Perce began. "It seemed like we'd better tell you about it. Mrs. Earnshaw doesn't like the sound of it. I think she may be right."

"More fighting?" I asked anxiously.

"No. quite the opposite," replied Mrs. Earnshaw grimly. "I can't understand it at the moment, but it seems the Reverend Blood is leading his flock on some sort of . . . pilgrimage, this evening."

"Pilgrimage? Where to?"

"Anchor Pool," she said quietly.

I was puzzled. This didn't make sense—but then it didn't strike me as particularly dangerous, unless . . . No. The thought that occurred to me was monstrous—out of the question.

"We're not happy about it," John Talbot said. "There's a funny mood abroad. Maybe Mrs. Earnshaw's told you something about it. All pawns in a universal game of chess, sort of thing. The individual has become . . . submerged. People don't talk about themselves any more; it's always 'we'. 'We of Riverside.' 'We humans.' It's like a Union meeting back on Earth, except running through it is this queer religious motif."

"They worship the water," said Alan Phipps bluntly. "They don't say it in so many words, but that's what it is." He was trembling, reliving the horror of his father's death. "They worship the stinking water, for Christ's sake! They're all going down to Anchor Pool this evening instead of having a service in church, and they're going to thank the damned water for blessings received. I know! I overheard them!"

"Alan has been listening in at the church," Mrs. Earnshaw explained. "I thought it best to know what was going on. Nobody says much to us any more."

"Do you know whose idea this is, Alan?" I asked.

"The Reverend announced it, but how do we know it's his idea? How does anybody know?"

I took his point. I began to get scared.

I was thinking of the lemmings again.

I was thinking of the fatties, leaving the security of their pens to swim to their death among the snapping teeth of the blackfish, swimming willingly, gladly.

I remembered the emanation of gratitude, faintly sensed that night. Pawns in the Cosmic Purpose. An alien ecology, intruded into by Man. Adaptation . . . There were no land carnivores on Arcadia, except Man . . . The symbiotic relationship between the Minds and the blackfish—the blackfish protected the Minds during the breeding cycle, but what did they receive in return?

An emanation of gratitude, a plethora of fatties beckoned irresistibly to the estuary. . . .

And the Reverend Blood, leading his flock of zombies to the water. . . ?

We discussed the matter; we made our plans. Alan Phipps was despatched back to the colony to fetch Miss Cotter, Minty, Yong and Spark. We needed every hand we could get. Within three hours they were back at the beach, after a detour to Farmer Blackstone's place. We rowed out to *Carousel*. We split up and boarded the trawlers, having left Jane, Miss Cotter, and old Annie to report on events on land with my two-way radio.

Jane hadn't spoken a word to me. When we left her on the beach she gave me a curiously defiant stare.

The rest of us then set off, a fleet of four boats, to attend the Anchor Pool thanksgiving service.

NINETEEN

We proceeded in line astern, moving swiftly up the estuary on the incoming tide. Perce led the way in his twenty-ton *Arcturus* with John Talbot as crew, followed by myself and Tom Minty in *Carousel*, then Mrs. Earnshaw and Alan Phipps in Eric Phipps' 15-tonner, with Yong and Spark bringing up the rear in an ancient 12-tonner owned jointly by sundry private colonists. As the trawlers puttered over the darkening water it was noticeable that the flying spray contained far less phosphorescence—just the occasional bright sparkle flung from under the bows like a glowing ember spat from a furnace.

When we moved between the headlands the tall cliffs cut off the sun's last rays; the opposite cliff was capped with a crimson corona as the shafts of light met the glittering granite. It was a beautiful sight, had we been in the mood to enjoy it. As it was, my appreciation was mingled with scepticism as I imagined the effect it would have on Blood and his flock. The sun would be shining straight into their eyes as they prayed around the pool, which itself would be glowing golden, a cosmic image of hope and rebirth. I supposed that Blood, or the Minds, had worked this out already.

The tidal flow was nowhere near as strong as it had been, and glancing at the dusk-bleached sky swept with cirrus, I could see only four moons—Aleph, Daleth, He, and Vau, if my recognition was accurate. In a few days the balancing effect of the scattered moons would reassert itself and Arcadia would once more experience its normal irregular, but slight, tidal rise and fall.

Minty read my thoughts. "Almost back to normal, Professor," he observed. "Once tonight is over, we can take it easy again." The Relay Effect was very slight now, but I caught a sadness from his mind. Knowing this, he continued ruefully: "And me

153

Syzygy

and the lads can go back to being the scapegoats. In a week or two we'll have forgotten what it's like to be the good guys. In fact, I doubt if folk will ever realize we *were* the good guys. All they'll remember is that we worked against the rest of them, as usual. Ah, well . . ." He sighed and hung over the rail, watching the following boats.

The startlingly harsh voice of Miss Cotter rasped through the radio. "I can see lights," she reported. "I'm up by the outcrop now, above Anchor Pool. I think they're on their way. Annie's sitting down by the pool, and Jane's gone back to the colony to check with anyone left behind. She says she may be able to get some extra help. Out!" The transceiver went dead. I got the impression that Miss Cotter was enjoying herself.

I wondered exactly what would be the general attitude of the colonists afterwards. Would they snap out of it, realize that they had been possessed or at best misled, and shower grateful thanks on their saviours? I didn't think it very likely. More probably, as Minty surmised, they would come to with the vague feeling of having been opposed and prevented from doing something which their emotions told them was right and proper. . . .

Always assuming that, after this evening, there would be a colony. . . .

Ahead, Perce was throttling back, and the mist of spray from his bows was subsiding. Soon he was wallowing in a wide arc, losing way; I heard a rattle as he dropped anchor and came to rest slightly downstream of the pool and about thirty yards offshore. I anchored a few yards behind him and the rest of the fleet did likewise. Soon the creek was silent, as the waiting boats rocked gently on the rippling water.

I looked shoreward. The shadows of the boats reached across the dark water of the pool, an angular blackness on the indigo. Beyond, the confused strewn boulders of the rockfall tumbled from the skyline to the water's edge, softened by the occasional tree or shrub and gilded by the sun. The wafting webs of the kite-bugs sparkled like stars. I dropped my gaze to the pool again and wondered what was happening down there, what dying thoughts were drifting through that short-lived Mind. There were faint emanations, and I caught again the sense of gladness, of gratitude, and, knowing what I knew, I tried not to be revolted by the cold logic of the Mind's reasoning. I could not expect empathy from an intelligence that was totally individual and unused to any type of cooperation save in its symbiotic relationship with the blackfish. The Mind cared nothing for human lives. Why should it? It could only deal with Humanity on the basis of the danger it represented, or the possible use to which it might be put. . . .

Tom Minty murmured something and pointed. I followed his finger and saw, away to the left, lights moving among the dense trees near the skyline. They grew closer, jerking and swinging as the colonists picked their way among the boulders and descended to the shore. I heard the occasional voice calling, directing; the lamps were switched off as their owners emerged from the gloom of the forest onto the golden sunlit rockfall. I turned and glanced across the river behind us; at this point it was wide, and the opposite hill low and flat. I calculated that there was a bare half-hour of sunlight left.

The emanations had changed subtly. The Relay Effects had strengthened, and I sensed a confused babble of thoughts overlaid with a slight feeling of bewilderment, but offset by a strong community spirit. These people were together. We, on the boats, our receptiveness and obedience deadened by drugs, were the outsiders. I had an irrational moment of sorrow when I knew that I did not belong, but I fought it back, knowing it was induced by the Mind. I could almost sense the Mind summoning up this final effort, its powers waning as its life drew to a close. I guessed that it could no longer compel all these people to obey its will, but with the assistance of the Relay Effect and a spirited address from the Reverend, it could achieve the same effect. . . .

The Reverend stood on the shore, an unmistakable birdlike figure in his flowing robes. Behind him, the boulders were covered with seated colonists, a huge audience rising like an amphitheatre to the jagged skyline. Blood spread his arms suddenly, the sleeves of his cassock hanging like wings, and the crowd became hushed. I saw Will Jackson remove his hat and noticed, inconsequentially, that he was totally bald. Blood turned towards the river, and we saw his face for the first time. The expression was curiously blank; he gave no acknowledge-ment of the boats' presence. He strode forward, stepping nimbly from rock to rock until he stood on the little island where Arthur, Jane and I had attempted to converse with the Mind.

Then he turned and faced his flock once more, spreading his arms again. The atmosphere was dense with an emission of awe; to those people on the rocks, dazzled by the setting sun, it must have looked as though Blood had walked on the water. I caught an image of him from their minds—a huge Godlike figure, a giant shadow in the setting sun that gilded his hair like a halo.

But I had no illusions about the Reverend's act. I knew what the audience saw and I knew what I saw, despite the powerful emanations of worship. He was good, but he was two-dimensional—a straight line from himself to his listeners. There was no depth to it; from the boats we saw a weak man temporarily strengthened by possession, but a weak man nevertheless. If I had any fear that the occupants of the fleet of boats would fall under his influence, I lost it as Minty spoke.

"What a load of crap," he remarked. "He's talking shit. Surely they're not swallowing all this?"

They were, judging by the rapt silence of that crowd on the boulders as Blood's voice rang up the hillside. ". . . this great communal act of worship, made voluntarily at a time when lesser men would be cringing in their homes, flinching from imaginary dangers . . . Yes, imaginary, my friends, because danger cannot exist where the overall Purpose is truly served. It is not fear of danger, that emotion which sends certain of our brothers fleeing for safety; it is selfishness, the selfishness of little men who think they are alone in the Galaxy. . . ."

Yes, he was getting through to his audience. I had expected this, but it was nevertheless depressing to see a large mass of people held spellbound by a load of cant. I blamed the Mind, but at the back of my thoughts was the uneasy feeling that it was always like this, Mind or not—that the Relay Effect merely strengthened the crowd's inborn eagerness to swallow opinions shouted by a vehement orator.

All my life it had been like this—I was always on the outside, as it were, looking in. A natural bloody-mindedness made me unsuited for communal activity. I wondered what was wrong with me. . . .

I realized that the Mind was getting at me, slyly.

I realized this in time, and at that moment I was reminded that I was not alone after all. There was a shout from the boat occupied by Yong and Spark.

"Crap!" they yelled in unison, in a manner which a few weeks ago, I would have considered a typically insolent example of their behaviour. Now I was glad of the touch of sanity. "Crap!" they repeated, taking up the rhythm with thumps of a deck-swab. "Crap, crap, crap! Blood E. L.! Blood E. L.! Crap, crap, crap!"

Beside me, Minty took up the cry and, farther away, I heard a harsh cackle of appreciation from Mrs. Earnshaw. Her cracked contralto joined the chant.

The Reverend increased his volume doggedly: "Living together on this alien planet we must realize, and I think I may say we do realize, our deep obligation towards the creatures which permit us . . ."

A blast on Perce's foghorn drowned him out. He wheeled round, robes whirling, his face twisted with fury. I saw his mouth working, but by now other foghorns had joned the chorus and the hills rang with a deep booming. I saw people on the bank rising from their boulders, and for a sick moment I thought we had gone too far, that the moment of absolution had been precipitated by our actions. Then I saw they were shaking their fists, gesticulating at us to be quiet.

I was watching the Reverend Blood. His expression had become strangely calm, and I think I saw him nod. A foreboding crept through my mind like a rising fog. And again the emanations came through—stronger, almost desperate. The dying Mind was making a last effort.

And there was nothing we could do. We stopped shouting, we stopped blowing the useless foghorns; we could only stand helpless as the Reverend, facing the crowd again, arms upraised, flung direct thoughts at them. Thoughts crystal clear and compelling, images as stereoscopic as sight. In a few moments he painted a mental picture of the Universe and Man's insignificance, then switched to Arcadia and the ocean, the inevitability of evolution and the status of Man in the general scheme of ecology. It was brilliant, vivid; it was a condensation of learning picked from the minds of every person there, evaluated and coordinated by the uncluttered, young-old intelligence of the Mind in Anchor Pool. It was presented perfectly to suit the slanted reasoning of the audience, who had already been indoctrinated for several days. I speak for myself—I don't know about the other occupants of the boats—but I do know that, in those moments, I was very nearly convinced. . . .

But the drug prodded me back to reality, and mentally I shook myself, slipped into the cabin, and carried out the dynamite we had brought as a last, desperate resort. . . .

I wondered how long the fading Mind could keep this up. Already Blood's emissions were beginning to waver like an uncertain 3-V signal. He had to make his move soon. I fingered the dynamite, playing with the fuse nervously. The crowd had risen, moved forward to the very edge of the water, staring at Blood raptly as though he were a Messiah. . . .

We would have to use the dynamite. We would need to throw it into the centre of the pool. We were under thirty yards from the shore. A number of people might be killed in the blast.

Blood's emissions continued, growing in urgency as they waned in power. He was reaching his climax, the point where he called on his flock to make the ultimate sacrifice for the benefit of the Cosmic Purpose. . . .

I glanced along the row of boats and saw that the crews had got their explosives ready; they were watching me for a signal.

The surface of Anchor Pool was a glittering pattern of knife-edged waves as the dorsal fins of the blackfish cut the surface. . . .

The crowd was ready. They had attained a state almost of Nirvana; they were poised on the brink of the pool, ready to surge forward at Blood's command. . . .

"Look! Oh, my God, look!" A shout, almost a scream in the concentrated silence. The emissions from Blood faltered—only for a second, but long enough for heads to turn and look back, up the hillside, at the figure on the skyline.

Long-haired and golden in the dying sun's last rays, she stood gracefully on a rocky pinnacle, her skirt swaying in the light breeze. There was not a person there who did not recognize her as she turned, and stumbled, and fell from the outcrop, disappeared behind a boulder, emerged, rolling asprawl, was still, her face upturned, beautiful, framed in fine blonde hair. . . .

Sheila.

Silence, then a great, low moan of superstitious horror. I saw people crossing themselves and the receptive atmosphere was vivid, a starshell of blinding involuntary emotions. Minty's hand was on my elbow, gripping me, restraining me from jumping into the blackfish-infested water in an effort to reach that figure lying motionless on the hillside. I saw people scrambling, a terrified confusion among the boulders at the water's edge as they struggled to get away. I saw old Jed Spark fall, saw him groping for his stick as the crowd surged past and over him.

Further emissions, one of them a poignant sensation of guilt and belated regret and self-recrimination . . . I saw from the corner of my eye a splutter of light from one of the trawlers. Turning, I saw Mrs. Earnshaw and Alan Phipps locked in a swaying embrace. She was clutching for his hand; he held a stick of dynamite, the fuse sparkled . . . As I watched he broke free and ran for the stern; he stood there, the stick clutched to his chest. Mrs. Earnshaw watched helplessly for a second, then moved away, hurried to the bow and crouched in the shelter of the capstan.

I turned back; I couldn't watch. The crowd on the shore had thinned. Minty was still gripping me tightly. One or two people were approaching the figure sprawled among the rocks—approaching cautiously, slowly. The Reverend Blood stood like a statue on the little island of rocks, watching silently.

The emanations ceased abruptly, cut off suddenly at their crescendo like a blown fuse, and I became aware of the shouting, the terrified wailing. Something caught my eye in the pool—a stirring in the lighter patch of black, a few ripples, a grey shape appearing, surfacing slowly, glistening.

The Mind was dead. It bobbed gently to the surface like a spherical buoy, inert, burnt-out, a globe of useless flesh. I remember I noticed that it was transformed, that the tightly-knit mass of plankton had merged into homogeneous cellular matter—then, horribly, the blackfish attacked it, tearing and snapping, feeding noisily. . . .

A blinding flash of white light illuminated the scene with unnatural brilliance; the concussion was shattering. The stern of Phipps' trawler erupted into flame and flying debris; there was a few seconds' deafening silence, then I ducked as particles of matter began to rain about us. I saw the Reverend Blood stagger in the blast. A baulk of timber struck him on the shoulder and he spun around, flapping and windmilling his arms as he tottered on the brink of the pool. He screeched like a scared bird as he lost his balance and fell thrashing among the feeding blackfish. . . .

Yong and Spark had cast off. Ignoring the spread of black robes lying like a manta ray in the water, they drifted alongside the sinking trawler and assisted Mrs. Earnshaw to safety. I saw Spark glance at the pool; he shrugged and turned away, put his arm around the old lady and helped her into the wheelhouse.

The shore was almost deserted now. I saw the flickering of lights among the trees as the colonists crept home. I cast off, started up the motor, and ran *Carousel* gently to the bank. Minty and I jumped out and ran to the little group gathered around the fallen girl. Old Annie was there; she looked up as I approached.

"She's coming round, Professor," she said shakily. "Gave us all a scare for a while, she did. She'll be all right in a minute."

I knelt down, gently removed the blonde wig from Jane's head, and held her close.

TWENTY

We sat around the radio the following morning, listening anxiously for the news. Mrs. Earnshaw was there, and Miss Cotter. Minty had dropped in to suggest that I stand for the Colony Committee at the next election. A representative from the Research Station would be a good thing, and he seemed to think that between the two of us we stood a chance of out-arguing some of the blimps. He also wanted me to join him and his friends for a drink to celebrate the reopening of the Social Club. He seemed to have shaken off the effects of the previous night remarkably quickly—myself, I still felt in shock. I had already tried to see Jane, but the doctor had met me at her unit and told me she was sleeping; he would rather I called back in an hour or so.

The time signal sounded, then the depressing notes of Arcadia's uninspired anthem.

The announcer's words were somehow unreal, and the disasters he catalogued remote. It is a fault of the Arcadian broadcasting system that the announcers habitually run the whole gamut of emotions in their tone of voice, from insane falsetto excitement at the opening of a new road, through hard-hitting but studious neutrality at the football results, to suicidal bass depression when discussing the export figures and the Planetary Debt.

So when in sepulchral tones he enumerated the terrible toll of life that had taken place the previous night, I was unable to reconcile his words with reality. The facts were catastrophic; maybe in a day or so I would feel bad about them. As it was, I was merely able to register that in all coastal sub-colonies apart from our own there had been heavy casualties occasioned by semi-religious and other gatherings becoming infected with mass hysteria and walking into blackfish-infested waters.

Fortunately, in most instances the shock of seeing their

fellows attacked had snapped large numbers of people out of it and they had saved themselves, scrambling for the shore. The Government, however, assured the population that the danger was at an end and the Minds dead. The new drug, which had been boycotted by the vast majority of the population, had proved its effectiveness and would be issued earlier at the next onset of the Relay Effect. If that was any consolation . . . There need be, therefore, no panic demands for emigration to other planets. Tomorrow was declared a day of mourning. The Premier would address the people after the evening news. A talk by Dr. Arthur Jenkins would follow.

I remember feeling irritated that we were the "population" when we walked into the sea or foolishly refused the drug, but became elevated to the status of "people" by the fact of being addressed by the Premier. Otherwise, the news that morning had very little emotional effect on me.

I switched the radio off. I couldn't bring myself to listen to Arthur's talk. I was certain that it would have been vetted by the authorities and would therefore contain little or no reference to the mishandling of the affair by the Government. Rather, the blame would be placed on the people for, I imagined, their lack of co-operation. After a suitable period had elapsed and the psychiatric teams were on their long journey back to Earth, the blame would be shifted again—subtly, because of the forthcoming election. Then Arthur and the various teams would come under fire as the experts, brought in at great expense, who had failed. . . .

Until eventually, in a few years, when the observers chronicled the events with the advantage of hindsight, it would be admitted that the incompetence was that of Mankind. . . .

Mrs. Earnshaw felt the same. "I can't work myself into a depression over a string of figures," she said. "What really upsets me is that it was all so unnecessary. The whole problem was mismanaged right from the start. After all, in a sense we're guests on this planet. We must expect inconveniences, and when they arise, it's no use blaming the plankton's breeding cycle, or the moons, or whatever. These things have been going on for millennia—but we've been here for a little over a hundred years. Everybody knew that, yet everybody made the same mistake of trying to flout evolution. Maybe we've learned now, but look at the cost . . . So next time let's hope they accept from the start that it's Man's fault, that it's Man who's not properly equipped to deal with his environment, and take steps to equip him accordingly, instead of trying to wipe out the opposition."

I agreed with her. "All the evidence was there to see," I pointed out. "Although it's a bit late to say that now. We never really wondered why there are no carnivorous animals on Arcadia. Now we know that once every fifty-two years any animal that doesn't include the drug plant in its diet is likely to be wiped out . . . You know, even our imported cattle adapted better than ourselves."

Tom Minty laughed. "Never mind, Professor. Next time they'll have us all doped to the eyeballs long before the Effect hits."

"I won't be here to see it," said Mrs. Earnshaw softly. "But I hope they do, for everyone's sake. I still can't forget that the drug's illegal, like all similar drugs since that business on Earth years ago . . . Now that the Minds have gone, there's no need to legalize it. So it won't be mass-produced until fifty-two years from now, and meanwhile you can take it from me they'll be working out all sorts of weird plans to counter the Minds; and they'll come up with some pretty good schemes, on paper. And by the time they've tried them out, and found they don't work, it's just possible they'll be too late again. . . ."

"Possible," agreed Minty. "I'll make sure I've got my supply handy. But I reckon they'll have to legalize it, Mrs. E. It grows everywhere. There's no way they can stop people from using it. I reckon that by the time the Minds start again we'll find that pretty near everyone has adapted, as it were, and we won't have any problem.

"But do you know what really scared me last night?" he went on. "It was standing there with the dynamite and thinking I might have to use it. Not because of killing a few people, maybe; bugger them, it was myself I was thinking of. Just suppose I'd lit the fuse and the Mind had stopped me from throwing it in. I kept thinking of poor old Clarke. . . ."

"You've got no confidence in your own drug, Tom," I said, "I think you'd have thrown it. The Mind was dying. It used all its power in the last effort to get the blackfish fed, and when Jane appeared, the sudden change of emotion caused it to blow.

Holding four hundred people like that, willing them to commit suicide, then to have to switch to a different group of people with different motives—the Mind couldn't have handled it. A week ago it might have tried, but the Arcadian animals have proved that the drug's a pretty good insurance against direct compulsion from the Mind, as well as being a perfect counter to the Relay Effect."

"Glad we didn't have to put it to the test," said Minty. He became aware that Mrs. Earnshaw and Miss Cotter were gathering up their possessions preparatory to moving out, and stood. "Can I give you a hand, Mrs. E?" he asked.

She smiled. "You're not such a bad lad as you try to have us think, Tom," she said. "Maybe the experience has changed some of us for the better. That includes me, I hope."

"I'm sorry, Jane," I said for the umpteenth time. "Will you forgive me?"

She regarded me coldly. "I might, perhaps. Sometime." Then the effort of acting became too much for her and she grinned suddenly. "Right now, perhaps," she said.

I bent over the bed and kissed her lightly, then kissed the bandage around her brow. "Does it hurt much?" I asked.

"Not now . . . It was a damned silly thing to happen, Mark. I just meant to put in an appearance. Make an entrance, sort of thing. But when they all saw me up there the emanations hit my mind like a bomb exploding, in spite of the drug, and I went dizzy for a second. I never intended the performance to be so realistic."

"I'll say it was realistic," I agreed. "There was one person who appreciated every detail . . . At least, it saved us having to use the dynamite. I was worried about that. We could have killed as many people as we saved. Imagine it, throwing the stuff from under thirty yards away in the hope that we could blast the blackfish and the Mind in the last instant before the Reverend persuaded his sheep to take to the water. It was a crude idea, but I couldn't think of anything better. Now, your idea . . . That was a touch of genius, my darling."

She regarded me doubtfully. "Do you think so? Well, if you say so. . . ."

And I wasn't going to say any more about it. Of course, I

knew the true reason why she had arrived at the outcrop at that moment, dressed in Sheila's clothes, wearing the long blonde wig. She had picked the only time available when she knew the assembled colonists, myself and the Mind would be present at the same time. She was desperate; she knew this was her only chance to elucidate, once and for all, the circumstances surrounding Sheila's death.

She would dress up as Sheila, she would appear dramatically at an emotional moment, she would shock a mental confession out of the person concerned in her sister's death, which by means of the Mind would be transmitted to every person there, including myself. At the same time she hoped to clear my mind of any doubts concerning Sheila.

And she succeeded. . . .

I don't think anyone in the colony will ever talk about it. So far as Riverside is concerned, the matter is best forgotten, buried with the many other tragedies of that eventful month.

But we will remember—I will remember—that vivid sequence of images from Alan Phipp's memory as he watched the reincarnation of Sheila, and lit the fuse of suicide.

The first part is conjecture. Sheila, suspicious following a conversation with Jane, sympathizing with my views on poaching, decides to do a little detective work on her own and takes a walk in the dark along the track to the point. On the way, she hears a not-unexpected explosion.

Then from Phipps' memory, the images . . . Cold water, naked, he wades about the pool gathering the stunned fish. Suddenly Sheila, watching him from the bank. The accusation. The fish, ignored, floating downstream as he struggles from the pool. Sheila moves away, climbs towards the path, announcing her intention of reporting him immediately. Her word against mine, thinks young Phipps, knowing that he can reach the colony before her, creep into his parents' unit, and pretend to be asleep when Officer Clarke comes knocking. . . .

But his clothes are not there; she has taken them as evidence, forseeing his plan. Alarmed, he gives chase, scrambling naked among the rocks.

And then the terrible, unnecessary fall, crystal clear in the images from his mind. Sheila runs along the outcrop; Phipps is a yard behind her—all he wants to do is reason with her, get his clothes back and talk it over. . . .

He grabs her, she pulls away, stumbles as a sticker plant gropes for her ankles, and goes over the edge. He hears her falling among the rocks; he climbs down, finds her dead. He searches for his clothes; he thinks they must be in her bag but he can't find it in the dark. Terrified, he goes home; he creeps through the streets nude, lets himself into the unit, where his parents are asleep. By the time the body is discovered the worral has hidden the bag. . . .

I've thought over this episode a lot, mulling over the facts and suppositions, always coming back to the final point of real tragedy, the moment of revelation at Anchor Pool.

Because the worst charge that Phipps could have faced was manslaughter. There was no question of murder. Yet, knowing this, he committed suicide. . . .

This is the tragedy. This is Arcadia.

The population of our planet is very small. Justice can only be implemented by Earth standards—these are the best we have, until someone comes up with something better. So . . .

What does a man do in a tiny community when he emerges from jail after ten or fifteen years, supposedly free? Where does he hide his past? Who gives him work? Where in the name of heaven does he *go*, after he walks out of those iron gates?

The law states that life imprisonment on Arcadia is for a maximum term of fifteen years. The facts I submit, state otherwise.

"So serious, darling?" said Jane. "Are you thinking of making an honest woman of me?"

I smiled, secure in the present, in Jane's bedroom. "I haven't had a chance to make a dishonest woman of you yet."

"My head feels fine," she said. "You've got your chance."

EPILOGUE

Three months later the Riverside Ladies' Circle decided, with some trepidation, to hold a dance, the proceeds to go to the Coastal Disaster Fund. No effort was spared in order to assure the success of the event. A well-known Master of Ceremonies was obtained. The band was a local group renowned for the shattering power of their amplifiers. Jane persuaded me to attend; it seemed that everyone was going. The dance was symbolic of Riverside's resumption of normal life, and of a new relationship between the Research Station and the private colonists. . . .

There was an unusual occurrence at about midnight. The atmosphere had been constrained at first; people felt a vague guilt at openly enjoying themselves, but later their reluctance had been submerged in drink and there was every sign that the night was going to be a success. The M.C. contributed a great deal towards the gradual thawing; he bellowed, his spectacles flashed hypnotically in the footlights, he willed people to have a good time.

He announced the Worral. "The latest sensation, Ladies and Gentlemen, our very own dance! Get twitching! Everybody on the floor!"

In the brief moment between the roar of acclamation and the band's first note, a voice was heard to ask, loudly and distinctly: "Why?"

There was a puzzled pause, but the band saved the day, launching with a mind-wrenching jangle of guitars into the insistent rhythm of the Worral.

People twitched, twitched in unison to the throbbing beat; but I noticed that large numbers were still sitting, drinking thoughtfully. Jane and I left early; she said that the guitars were giving her a headache.

On the following pages are details of some Arrow Books that will be of interest:

THOMAS M. DISCH (editor)

THE RUINS OF EARTH

Cities choked by killer smog. Freeways clogged with autojunk. Nature running down – societies in crisis.

Man is at last waking up to the terrible damage he is inflicting on his environment. The various routes to disaster have already been charted.

But the damage still goes on.

This collection of stories by leading science fiction writers – each committed to a human vision of society – attempts to take the ecological inquiry one stage further. To indicate *why* we are destroying our world – and what the possible consequences for us all may be.

PHILIP STRICK (editor)

ANTIGRAV

Stories to lift you straight out of this world! Are you ready to meet an elephant with a wooden leg? A Martian who has married your daughter? An entire island of beautiful girls just waiting for your touch? A house that spies on you when you go to bed?

Be warned! ANTIGRAV is a collection of incredible stories from today's topmost writers of science fiction. And they've made some discoveries you won't believe – until they happen to you.

JAMES BLISH

CITIES IN FLIGHT: his famous science fiction quartet

THEY SHALL HAVE STARS

A.D. 2018 – the Cold Peace, worse even than the Cold War with bureaucratic regimes in Washington and Moscow indistinguishable in their passion for total repression. But in the West, a few dedicated individuals still struggle to find a way out of the trap of human history.

A LIFE FOR THE STARS

The world's natural resources have long been exhausted and city after city goes 'Okie' – lifts off the earth to earn its living among the stars.

EARTHMAN, COME HOME

When the cities left earth, they moved into a constantly changing environment. In a multi-cultural universe an iron hand was needed to impose order upon the spaceways.

A CLASH OF CYMBALS

Earth is finished as a galactic power. Now, from the heart of the Milky Way, come the first tentative strands of the Web of Hercules – the strange culture that is destined to be the next great civilization of the galaxy.

STANISLAW LEM

SOLARIS

The planet Solaris in the constellation of Alphia in Aquarius.

The planet that has given rise to a new branch of science – solaristics. The planet on which a permanent watch was mounted. A space-station that hovered above the mysterious ocean of Solaris. An ocean apparently sentient, its substance unknown, an ocean possibly 'alive', although that all depended on how you defined 'life'. An ocean that definitely reacted on occasions to external stimuli.

And the 'others' that Kelvin discovered on the space-station? 'Others' that had driven a predecessor to suicide. Hallucinations? Projections of the scientists' imaginations? Or another manifestation of the ocean's powers?

If you would like a complete list of Arrow books please send a postcard to
P.O. Box 29, Douglas, Isle of Man, Great Britain.